Confessions of a
Naughty Night Nurse

LILY HARLEM

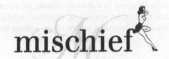

mischief

Mischief
An imprint of HarperCollins*Publishers*
77–85 Fulham Palace Road,
Hammersmith, London W6 8JB

www.mischiefbooks.com

A Paperback Original 2013

First published in Great Britain in ebook format by
HarperCollins*Publishers* 2012

Copyright © Lily Harlem 2013

Lily Harlem asserts the moral right to
be identified as the author of this work

A catalogue record for this book is
available from the British Library

ISBN-13: 9780007553341

Find out more about HarperCollins and the environment at
www.harpercollins.co.uk/green

Contents

Contents

Chapter One

'He's dead.'

'Ah shit, another one?'

'Yep, bless him, it was peaceful, though.'

'That's the third this week, isn't it?'

'Yeah, so that should be us done for a while now; they come in threes.'

The two staff nurses talking over a body in sideward six were hunched forward, with shadows spreading out behind them. A tap dripped in the corner, a musty smell hung in the air, and the wind rattled past the lead-paned window.

I stepped closer and cleared my throat.

They both turned.

'Sharon, are you here for us?' Annie asked with a smile. Her auburn hair, roughly pinned in a bun, wobbled as she spoke.

'Yes. Please say you're expecting me. I'm fed up of being passed from pillar to post this week.'

'Too right we are. We're so short here tonight, and now this, another trip to Rose Cottage.'

I fastened my fob watch onto my uniform, just over my left breast. 'I'll go.'

She widened her eyes. 'Are you sure? It's bloody awful out there.'

I shrugged, feigning nonchalance. I never refused a trip to the mortuary – or Rose Cottage as it was known, so as not to offend delicate dispositions. 'Yeah, whatever, I'm here to help out and I've got a coat.'

She glanced at her colleague, pulled down the edges of her mouth, then looked back at me. 'Cheers then, that's great.'

Her colleague, whom I didn't know, but had Staff Nurse Nancy Tinkard written on a brass badge, tugged the sheet over the slackly wrinkled face on the bed, covering the unseeing, half-open eyes but leaving a tuft of grey hair sticking out. She reached up and turned off the saline drip. 'We'll give it the usual hour of respect before we come back in here then,' she said.

'Do you have a report card I can use?' I asked.

'Sure, I'll get you one.' Tinkard opened the window the tiniest crack, and a hiss of wind whistled in. She then stepped past me and out of the sideward.

I followed her up the dimly lit ward, a rise of anticipation growing in my belly and my pulse picking up a notch. Rose Cottage always meant a few minutes' fun on an otherwise dull night. It wasn't The Ritz and they didn't bother with home comforts like mattresses and pillows for their guests, but hey, I could cope.

'Have you just joined the hospital?' I asked.

'Yeah, moved up from Sheffield to live with my boyfriend in Skipton,' she said over her shoulder.

'Enjoying it?'

'It's OK, apart from the fact it's nearly ten and the house officers haven't been round yet.'

'I know, makes you wonder what they teach the junior doctors these days.' I suppressed a laugh. Here ten would be early for house officers to make their final rounds. She must have been spoilt with eager, efficient doctors wherever she'd worked before.

We sat at a long white desk with a hidden artificial light shining from a plinth above onto the surface.

'Here you go,' she said, 'we have a full house, well, apart from Mr Parslow's bed when he's gone.' She passed me a sheet of paper with every resident on the geriatric ward, named, aged and diagnosed. 'Then we'll have one, for emergencies, but Heathcliff Ward have three empty, so if Iceberg, or whatever you lot call senior night nurse Lisa Stanton rings, be sure to tell her how busy we are here.'

'Absolutely.' I glanced down the list. There was no patient less than eighty-four and no one for resuscitation should they decide to stop breathing or their heart gave up.

Footsteps caught my attention, the sharp click of heavy leather soles taking long strides on linoleum flooring.

'Hey, ladies, how are you doing?'

'Hi, Carl.' I grinned. 'Why are you out of your surgical hole?'

He set his hands on the desk, stooped, and his red stethoscope swung from around his neck. 'Covering for sickness,' he said with a shrug.

'About time you got here.' Tinkard slapped several drug charts on the table next to his fingers. 'We've got drugs to be written up, three warfarins, and now there's one to pronounce too, in sideward six.'

Carl tugged his gaze from mine and flashed her one of his most charming smiles. 'I'm really sorry. It's been hell in A&E all afternoon and then I had to assist in surgery. Got to do the day job on top of the extra-curricular care-of-the-elderly fun.'

Tinkard tutted. 'Well, what am I supposed to do now? Wake up my patients to take evening medication?'

'Yeah, I suppose so.' He straightened, pulled a black pen from his pocket, jabbed in the end and released the ballpoint with a flamboyant click. 'You got the blood results then?'

Tinkard was already holding them in the air, wafting them like tissue paper.

Carl grabbed them. 'Cheers.'

He glanced at me and I knew he was doing his best

4

to be patient. Behind his square, black glasses he had rings under his eyes, his tie was skew-whiff and there was a blob of what was either blood or Bolognese on his white coat. Goodness only knew how many hours he'd been on his feet.

Tinkard pulled a rattle of keys from her pocket and wandered off, towards the clinical room, her footsteps perfectly silent.

Carl took her vacated seat, folding his long body into the low plastic chair and tucking his knees beneath the desk. 'You picked the short straw tonight then, working with "Nurse Happy"? God knows where she turned up from.'

'She's OK, she just cares about her patients.'

'Yeah, I suppose. Trouble is I have to prioritise bleeding oesophageal varices over a few warfarin write-ups.'

'Oh dear, not nice. Any luck?'

'Yeah, he's in intensive care. Puts you off booze, though.'

'Was he a soak?'

'Yes, sixty units a week.'

'Impressive by anyone's standards.' I glanced at my fob watch. 'You got your car back yet?'

'Yes, they managed to get the dink out of it without too much problem. Last time I go to the supermarket on a windy day, though. Bloody trolleys blowing about all over the place.'

'You'll be hungry then, this weather is set in for a few months. That's how it is in the Dales.' I tried and failed to stifle a yawn, waggling my hand in front of my mouth. 'Sorry, I'm knackered, as usual.'

'Me too, can't wait for my days off. I'm just going to sleep.'

An image of him sprawled in bed, limbs tangled in sheets, hair messy, glasses off, came to my mind. I would eventually get into his bed with him, or have him up against a wall, over a trolley or even in a linen cupboard. Carl was a hottie in a nerdy-but-flirty kind of way, and we were playing an unspoken game of let's-see-how-long-we-can-resist-banging-each-other-stupid. It was fun, this dancing around in a horny-doctor, sexy-nurse ritual. And let's face it, he was fresh out of med school, five years of study, study, study, and now he'd been let loose in a hospital. He needed some action of the non-clinical variety and a lesson on how the land lay in the jungle.

A red light flashed on the dash screen, signalling a patient needed a nurse in bay four. Standing, I lightly pressed Carl's shoulder. 'See you later.'

He shoved his hand through his dark, slightly too-curly hair and looked up. 'Hopefully not.' He suddenly frowned. 'Not that I don't like seeing you, I do. But I really want to get some kip after this.'

'I know what you mean, don't worry.'

As I walked away I knew he was checking out my bum.

His gaze was hot on my buttocks and had been getting hotter ever since I'd accidently-on-purpose shown him the top of my black stockings last week when helping a patient out of bed. Now I didn't need to showcase my hosiery to get him worked up, he knew it was there; ten denier sheerness, then delicate lace that was strikingly dark against my pale, sun-starved flesh.

'Hey, Mr …' I glanced at the notes at the base of the bed. '… Watkins, did you need something?'

'I don't know you.' Mr Watkins' big blue eyes peered up at me and his gnarled fingers clutched a starched sheet beneath his chin.

'I'm Sharon, one of the nurses looking after you.'

'Where am I?'

'On Bronte Ward.'

'Bronte Ward, where's that?' His hold on the sheet tightened and the bulging blue veins that threaded over the backs of his hands twitched.

'You're in hospital, on Bronte Ward.'

'No, I'm not. I'm waiting … for them.' He narrowed his eyes, the skin at the corners pinching, as he darted his gaze left to right. 'I have a weapon, you know.'

I flicked on the night light, hoping it would help orientate him, and glanced at my report card to see if he had dementia. No, just a urine infection which often made older people confused until the antibiotics kicked in. 'Who is them?' I asked, smiling down.

'The Germans, they're coming here, tonight.'

I rested my hand over one of his and noted how cool his flesh was. 'No one is coming here tonight, especially not Germans,' I said. 'Everyone is tucked up in bed and you're quite safe.'

He hesitated. 'Are you sure?'

'Absolutely, now how about I get you a nice cup of tea?'

'Can you do that? Are you allowed? What if the Germans see the light of the fire?'

'They won't, I promise. Do you take sugar?'

'Well, I would if it wasn't rationed, six of the buggers. Nothing like sweet tea to get you through the night.'

I bit my lip to stop myself retorting that I enjoyed plenty of other sweet treats to get me through my working night. But I didn't want to confuse Mr Watkins further.

'Sharon, you said?' He eyed me with a fraction less suspicion.

'Sharon, that's right. I'm here to look after you. Now how about that cup of tea?' I straightened his pillow to support his neck better. 'It will warm you up. You feel a bit chilly.'

'Are you sure it's safe to make tea?'

'I'm sure.' Not the first time in my career, I hated how those distant years affected soldiers when they reached their end days. 'You really are safe here, nothing is going on tonight so I'll go and put the kettle on and then maybe, in a little while, you'll be able to settle down and get some rest.' I reached for the blanket folded over the end of the bed, shook it out and laid it over him. 'Is that OK?'

He studied my name badge with a lucidity in his expression I hadn't seen a few moments ago. 'Yes, that's fine, Miss Sharon Roane.'

'Great, I'll be back in a jiffy with that tea and ...' I leaned in, conspirator-like, 'I will make it as sweet as I can get away with.'

He twitched his mouth into a half smile. 'You will?'

'I will.'

'Just ...' He licked his dry lips. 'Be careful, you never know when they might jump out at you.'

The moment of clarity was slipping. 'I'll be careful, don't you worry.'

'Yes, keep low, stay in the shadows and don't give them any clues to your whereabouts.'

Waiting for the kettle to boil, I plucked out my iPhone and whizzed off a message to Tom.

Got one for you. Midnight-ish.

As I shook three sachets of Silver Spoon into the tea my phone chirped a reply.

Thank fuck. I was losing the will to live – the company here is deathly dull!

I smiled and slipped my phone away. The thought of Tom always gave me a thrill of anticipation, not to mention that I liked to make the most of his impressive body, and all of its generous assets, while I could.

After dodging Germans to take Mr Watkins his tea and another, warmer, blanket, I helped an old guy onto a commode, replaced several urine bottles – which included a battle with a particularly onerous waste-masher in the sluice – and changed an insulin syringe with Tinkard.

'You OK to take first break?' she asked, signing the drug chart and shoving it back in the folder. Her tone implied I had no choice, despite the guise of a question.

But I was used to this. First break was the worst and as a bank nurse, going to whichever ward was short because of illness, holidays or lack of employable staff in the Dales, I always got stuck with it. The trouble with taking the first two hours was it was too early to crave sleep and too early to have the munchies so it made the rest of the shift so damn long. 'Yeah, OK,' I said with a shrug. I could have argued, made a fuss, but what was the point? Besides, tonight it might just work in my favour.

Mr Parslow was, of course, waiting when Annie, the auburn-haired staff nurse, and I finally headed into side-ward six.

'You want to wash or dry?' she asked.

'I'll dry.' May as well save my over-scrubbed hands from water time.

She set the soapy bowl on the table and wheeled it close. Dumped in a wad of disposable flannels.

I lifted the sheet from Mr Parslow. He wore a pair of stained pyjama bottoms and a white string vest. 'Are we taking this out?' I asked, indicating the cannula in the back of his right hand.

'Yeah, he was seen this morning by Javier, it was hardly an unexpected death.'

Plucking a roll of micropore from my pocket, I removed the plastic needle and applied a makeshift plaster for his bloodless skin with a ball of cotton wool. If deaths were unexpected or unexplained, an autopsy would be performed and that meant leaving any cannulas, catheters, or tubes where they were in case they'd contributed to the cause of death. Poor old Mr Parslow had simply died because his body had worn out with age.

'How old was he?' I asked.

Annie gently wiped his thin face. Not that it was dirty, but out of respect, to ensure he went to Rose Cottage clean and tidy. 'Ninety-three, not a bad innings.'

'I wouldn't complain.' Where she'd washed I dried with a blue-and-white striped towel. 'How come Javier was on geriatrics?' Dr Javier Garelli was a six-foot-two hunk of Italian muscle, his skin shone like bronze and he had cheekbones most supermodels would hurl themselves off the catwalk for. He worked in general surgery and as a senior house officer was Carl's immediate superior.

'Hartley's surgical team were covering. Not that the day staff had a problem with Javier being around, they said his aftershave lingered for well over an hour after he'd headed to Eyre Ward.'

'I'm sure.' His aftershave was divine, kind of sugary but masculine too, fresh air but with suggestion of a long, sultry night. It was like the rest of him, sexy as hell. What I wouldn't do to have my wicked way with him on a gurney one night.

'He's bonking Iceberg you know.'

My heart stuttered at this new bit of gossip and a rise of bile burned my chest. 'No way.'

'Yes way. Apparently they were caught in out-patients at two in the morning by a porter searching for a drip-stand.' Her gaze caught mine and her eyes flashed. She had the look of a kid at Christmas who'd pop if they didn't open their presents – now. 'Yeah, he had her bent over a table, her awful crinoline trousers around her ankles and was going for it, big time ...' her voice dropped to a whisper, 'up her bum.'

'Seriously?'

'Yeah, seriously.'

She tugged Mr Parslow's vest off his left arm and I did the same with the right, then we slipped it carefully over his head. As his bony skull settled back on the pillow I tried to close his eyes with my palm, but they slid back to half mast, unseeing and milky-glazed.

12

'Roll to me?' I asked.

Annie was already wringing out the flannel ready to wash his back. 'Yep.'

I tugged the frail body by shoulder and hip, exposing angled scapulae and prominent vertebrae. A huff of air, like a strangled groan, rattled up from his chest and scratched through his throat. I glanced downwards. His jaw had slackened a little further at the movement. 'Do you think the porter could be making it up? You know what they're like.'

'I don't know, it's a rumour, and rumours are like wildfire once they get started around here.' She washed his back quickly then dried with a flourish. 'But there's no smoke without fire and stranger things have happened than the hospital's number one stud getting up-hill action with the senior nurse.'

'I suppose.' I wondered what Javier could possibly see in Iceberg. She was a cold-hearted cow – everyone thought so. Last week she'd snapped at me for sitting down on the job when I'd gone off duty twenty minutes previously and was waiting for the rain to ease before heading home on my bicycle. Not bothering to listen to my explanation, she threatened to have my pay docked and inform Personnel of my inherent slackness.

I rested Mr Parslow onto his back again and rummaged in the bedside locker for clean pyjamas. Found some; navy and crisply new, with a Marks and Spencer price tag still in place. I wondered if whoever bought these had any idea they'd be the last clothes he'd ever wear. If so, it was nice that they were M&S, you could rely on the quality.

Annie had whipped off the existing pyjama bottoms and was washing his withered, lifeless penis with well-practised efficiency. 'Apparently he's off in March, got a registrar post at St George's.'

'In London?' I took up the task of drying where her flannel had been.

'Yeah, will serve Iceberg right if she falls for him then he goes and leaves her.'

I muttered an agreement and we dressed our silent patient in his smart, new pyjamas. Despite the quiet, reverent task I couldn't help the wave of panic in my guts. Javier had been working in my hospital for nearly two years and I hadn't once played hide-the-sausage with him. I always presumed there'd be plenty of time for that conquest. Part of me enjoyed the slow burn, the flirty smiles and suggestive banter we indulged in whenever our paths crossed in the dead of night. Another part of me now worried that I'd been wasting time when I could have been getting down and dirty, sweaty and naked, with my very own Italian stallion.

There was only one thing for it. I would have to up my game, become the hunter rather than the hunted.

Javier had no idea what was about to hit him, literally.

Mr Parslow was now fresh and dressed. Annie and I quickly tidied the room, did an inventory of his meagre belongings – splayed toothbrush, red comb strung with silver hairs, a half packet of toffees and several items of nightwear in various states of cleanliness – then we wrapped him in a paper-thin shroud and covered him with a clean sheet.

Annie left and I dropped the last of the damp towels into a linen skip.

A sudden bang on the window caught my attention. I turned and stared into the bleak darkness. The blind hadn't been drawn over the slightly open pane and a feathery flash of silver-white knocked up against the glass. Once, twice, three times.

Curious, I stepped closer, trying to discern what was buffeting the rain-splattered window with firm insistence.

A gasp of surprise caught in my throat. It was a dove, out at night, in a gale.

'What on earth are you doing?' I bent and peered closer.

A black, beady eye's attention settled on mine for the briefest of moments, then the dove took off, into the night, its wings ethereal and ghost-like, flapping against the wind.

I glanced at the mound on the bed and fought a prickle of unease tickling the back of my neck. Odd things happened in a hospital, but a dove, at night; that had been a first.

Quickly I shut the window. Mr Parslow's soul had had ample time to depart. All that remained was his shell, so there was no need to have an escape route for his spirit to start its journey to Heaven; and I was pretty certain it would be Heaven, what with having a white dove coming to collect him on a storm-wild night.

I didn't mention the dove to Annie or Tinkard. I just called for a porter to help me transfer to Rose Cottage and tugged on my coat. I checked my iPhone again. Another message from Tom.

You coming?

I typed back quickly.

Yes, so will you soon!

The porter appeared. He was new, a young guy, wide and stocky with hair so short you could see his scalp through it. He had the word *love* tattooed over the knuckles on his right hand.

'You got one for Rose Cottage,' he grunted, tugging the closed, coffin-style trolley along behind him.

'Yes, sideward six.'

Luckily Mr Parslow's skinny body was light, and within a few minutes we were heading out of the ward with him safely ensconced in the metal trolley.

'Hey, Sharon,' Tinkard called. 'You may as well go for your break after you've done that, it's just gone midnight.'

'Right you are.'

The ward door shut with a heavy click and I put some muscle into pushing the trolley along the deserted corridor. As the pace picked up I stared at the lumpy back of the porter's head and wondered if he was the one who'd found Javier and Iceberg.

If only I could see into his mind.

I pondered on whether I should question him. Just come straight out and ask if he'd seen the hottest medical senior house officer since Pompeii's hospital had got showered in ash, shagging the Wicked Witch of the West where the sun doesn't shine.

I thought better of it. My asking alone could become gossip, and I was keen to avoid gossip that included myself. There were too many skeletons in my cupboard, and, for that matter, in clinical rooms, sluices, linen rooms, and in that handy, unused office at the back of the pharmacy. No, I would keep quiet and do my own investigating.

Stepping out into the night, I was whipped in the face by my hair, the band holding it in a low ponytail no match for the ferocity of the gale. I hunched my shoulders and stooped, trying to shelter my face from the needle-points of rain blasting my cheeks. The sound of the torrent of drips hitting the metal trolley was almost as loud as the wind creaking at the row of oaks leading to Rose Cottage. Their boughs strained and moaned, their leaves hissing in great waves of noise.

17

The porter sped up behind the back of the canteen and put considerable energy into pulling. By the time we went past the incinerator and turned the final corner, I found myself jogging along the uneven path.

Luckily Tom was waiting with the door to Rose Cottage held open.

We rushed in, the trolley banging over the door-bar and a scurry of leaves whirling around our feet.

'Fucking hell,' the porter said. 'It's cold enough to freeze the balls off a brass monkey out there.'

Tom shut the door, winked at me, then took hold of my end of the trolley and wheeled it into the bay of body drawers. I trailed along behind, tucking my wind-wild hair back into its ponytail.

'Yeah, good job the VIPs in here don't care about shitty weather,' Tom said, stopping at twenty-six C and then opening the trolley's lid to reveal Mr Parslow's covered body.

'Bloody hate this part of the job, me,' the porter said, staring at the shroud-covered lump and shuddering. 'Don't think I'll ever get used to it.'

'You go if you want,' I said, 'I'll help here.'

He widened his eyes and took a step backwards. 'Really?'

'Sure, I've done it a million times. Doesn't bother me.'

'Bloody hell, thanks …' He nibbled on his bottom lip and scanned my coat, as though searching for my name badge.

'Sharon,' I said. 'Go, we've got this covered and I bet you've lots to do.'

'Yeah, I have actually.' He yanked his sleeves over his hands and strode back to the door.

Tom followed and I heard him lock it shut, as was standard procedure at Rose Cottage. The NHS couldn't risk body snatching, that's why Tom was employed as night security here.

'Poor sod,' Tom said, wandering back in. 'Looked white as a sheet, didn't he?'

'They all do to start with.'

Tom pulled open the drawer and together we slid Mr Parslow onto the metal; his body, although light, was a dense weight. Tom then pushed the drawer shut and closed the door with a resounding slam.

He wrote Mr Parslow's name on a piece of card and slipped it into a slot beneath.

'So how long have you got?' he asked, a naughty smile tugging his lips and his smoky-blue eyes twinkling.

I raised my eyebrows. 'No time at all. Change of plan, I have to get straight back, sorry.'

'Ah, Sharon,' he said, frowning. 'Why do you go and tease me like that? You know how much I look forward to your visits. They're the only thing that keeps me going in this lifeless place.'

'Sorry.' I glanced down his body. Through his uniform – dark-navy trousers and shirt – Tom's well-defined muscles could be made out, as could a fantastically long wedge of flesh behind his fly.

My pussy clenched as I remembered last week when I'd paid him a visit. He'd bent me over the desk and rammed himself into me for nearly an hour. It had been so damn hard to walk back onto the orthopaedic ward I'd actually considered nicking a pair of crutches.

I hitched in a breath, knowing I wouldn't be able to keep up my pretence for more than another few seconds. Tom's big dick and his skilful use of it was too damn irresistible. 'The ward is crazy busy.'

He reached for me but I stepped away. 'Just a kiss and a quick grope then, to keep me going.'

Quickly I moved even further away, towards the autopsy room. 'Ha, ha,' I said gleefully. 'Just kidding, I'm on my break now.'

He flattened his lips into a tight line, as if holding back a broad smile, though at the same time narrowing his eyes as though furious with me. 'You little minx,' he said. 'You'll pay for that.'

'Only if you can catch me.' I darted into the autopsy room, dark except for a couple of low lights over a set of huge scales. The air was cool and laced with disinfectant.

I glanced around. There was a big, steel surgical table in the centre, a row of cupboards, several filing cabinets and a desk holding an ancient computer monitor.

'Sharon,' Tom called, the door shutting behind him with a soft whoosh. 'You can't escape.'

'No, please, no,' I said with a giggle and ran towards the far side of the room.

He chased but I dodged at the last minute, went to run for the door. He cut me off and I swivelled, found myself barging into the bolted-down table in the middle.

I gasped as the air flew from my lungs, but recovered quickly and, with my hands flat on the cool surface, scooted to the end.

Tom was facing me now, his face strewn with shadows, but I could see the thrill of the chase had flushed his cheeks and caused him to pant.

'Come here,' he said, edging closer.

'No.' I moved away from him in a circle around the table.

But it was futile; he was tall, fast and strong. Suddenly I was grabbed and tugged to the end, my body pulled up against his.

He pressed his lips down hard on mine and instantly the game was over. Now it was all about carnal satisfaction. With Tom, I was always guaranteed a spectacular orgasm and I couldn't wait to start riding towards it.

'Ah, yeah, baby, I've got you,' he said, shoving my coat off and flicking it out of the way. 'You gonna take it good again? Like you did last week?'

21

'Yes,' I panted, tearing at the buttons on his shirt. 'Yes, that was so hot, I could hardly bloody walk the next day.'

He chuckled, low, deep and sexy, then kissed me again, the stubble on his chin scraping my skin and his breaths blowing hot and hard on my cheek.

He had my uniform up around my waist now and was forcing me to lie back on the ice-cold table. He stepped between my legs and leaned over me, pressing his groin into the gusset of my knickers.

'Really, on here?' I said, slotting my fingers into his hair and drawing my knees up so they pressed either side of his hips. 'Where they chop up dead people? Isn't that a bit freaky?'

'The French for orgasm is *petite mort* so it's kind of fitting.' He was fiddling with the elastic of my underwear, at the juncture of my thighs.

'Yeah, I suppose, but, oh –' My words were cut off and turned into a delighted moan. He'd plunged two fingers high up inside me and found my clit with his thumb.

'Oh, you're such a dirty nurse,' he murmured, kissing and licking over my cheek. 'I bet you've been getting wetter and wetter ever since that poor old sod croaked, haven't you?'

'I –' Words wouldn't come. My brain could only concentrate on his touch.

He pulled out a little, shoved back in and set up a steady rhythm. Small squelching noises echoed around

22

the room, mixing with my panting breaths and the sound of my pulse raging in my ears.

'I love it when you get so wet for me,' he said, gripping the back of my neck with his free hand and nibbling the side of my neck. 'I'm going to really miss your cream, Sharon.'

'Ah, yes, Tom, please, I want you in me.'

His hand was good, but a hand was a hand. Tom's equipment was sensational, the sort of specimen that should be pickled in a jar when he died and saved in a museum as a perfect example of the human penis.

'Coming right up, baby,' he said, withdrawing and fumbling with his flies.

I shoved at my knickers, gasped briefly at the chill on my buttocks, then kicked the material away. I tried not to think of the bodies that had lain lifeless where I was about to be screwed senseless. Perhaps it would re-balance the karma for this table – if furniture held karma, that is.

Tom was rolling a condom on with astonishing efficiency. 'You're the only one that ever takes all of me,' he said, looking me in the eye. 'And it feels amazing.'

'Tell me about it.' I reached for him and kissed him hungrily as he pressed me back onto the hardness of the metal. He tasted of coffee, chocolate and perhaps a hint of tobacco. He tasted of Tom, which to me meant sex and pleasure and orgasms of the super-intense variety.

He was nudging into me. I locked my ankles in the

small of his back and gripped the sleeves of his shirt. This part always required a good amount of concentration on my behalf if it was to be erotic pain and not ow-that-hurts pain.

'Yeah, that's it,' he said into my mouth and gaining the first inch of entry.

I held my breath, waiting for more, desperate for more, all of it, all of him.

'Damn, you feel so hot,' he said, pressing his chin against my temple.

His stubble would leave a telltale red rash, but I didn't care, to hell with any consequences. Right now I just wanted more of him inside me.

I rocked my hips up to meet him and he pushed in – much faster than usual.

'Oh, yes,' I cried out as red flashes filled my vision. 'So good.'

'Only good?' He stilled.

'Fantastic, and you know it.' I half-heartedly thumped his arm. 'Just give it to me.'

He hesitated for a second, then shunted in completely. I cried out, so did he.

The brutal entry and the swirling pleasure-pain had my entire body tensing.

'Ah, yeah,' he groaned, lifting his head and staring at the wall behind me. 'Fuck, yeah.'

I felt like I would burst. That at any moment the tip

24

of his cock would come right out of my throat. How was it possible for my little body to take such a monster? I didn't know, but it did, and it felt bloody incredible.

Tom began to move. Keeping himself lodged high, he churned his hips in a circular movement, catching my clit just right.

Groaning, I arched my back, lifted off the table and clung to him. Already the first blissful sparks of orgasm were there. It wouldn't take long.

'Ah, yeah, this isn't going to be a marathon session like last week,' he said. 'You've got me too damn hot for you. I'm near already.'

'Me too.' I smoothed my hands over his shoulders. 'Me too.'

He pulled halfway out, sliding easily, then rode back in. We both grunted and I harnessed the growing pressure.

'Yeah,' he said, repeating the process. 'Oh, yeah.'

'Faster, harder,' I said, catching his fleshy earlobe in my mouth and sucking.

'Your wish is my command.'

Suddenly our mating cranked up a notch. If it had been desperate before, now it was frantic, wild and utterly animalistic. Breathing no longer mattered, nor did the rest of the universe. Tom inside me and the explosion about to detonate was all that existed.

'Ah, I'm coming,' I shouted, biting down on his earlobe.

'Fuck, fuck, fuck,' he groaned, shifting his head but not escaping my teeth.

He was rod-hard, as hard as he ever got. And I was being impaled; he was ramming me down as much as he was forging into me.

It was there. I was spinning through ecstasy, my body not my own for a few sweeter-than-sweet seconds, but belonging to a glorious state of heavenly pleasure.

And then came the best bit, my pussy contracting and spasming around Tom's cock. My internal muscles rejoicing at the incredible length and girth they had to grip and shudder against.

Tom was coming too, at the perfect moment. He was groaning and moaning like a dying man. I released his ear, found his mouth and kissed him. He kissed back, hungrily.

'Oh, yeah, that was so good,' he said, breathless and finally slowing his thrusting hips.

'Tell me about it.' I was trembling, my flesh prickly and sweat-coated.

'You're incredible,' he said.

'Kind of you to say so.' I brushed his hair back from his face where it was hanging like dark fingers around his forehead. 'How are the wedding plans going?'

'Not bad, Cheryl is stressed but her mum's helping her.'

'It must be a nightmare planning such a big event for so many people.'

'Yeah, well, it's what she wants.'

He touched his nose to mine, rubbed it in an Eskimo kiss. 'Are you sure we can't still do this once I've tied the knot?'

'We've had this conversation before.' I stroked his earlobe – it was wet and slightly swollen from my exuberant kisses and bites.

'I know, but bloody hell, Sharon, we're so damn good together.' As if to prove the point he ground into me, extracting another delicious tremor. I couldn't hold in a satisfied groan.

'I have some morals, you know,' I said when I'd recovered, 'and screwing married men is definitely on my list of no-no's.'

'But how is this different? I'm engaged to be married right now.'

'You haven't promised to forsake all others yet, though, have you?'

'No, I suppose not.' He kissed me gently. 'I will miss this, though. You. Us.'

'Me too. But Cheryl makes you happy and will do for the rest of your life.'

'Yep, she's great.' He pulled out and straightened.

I became aware of the cold, unyielding surface I was lying on and the dampness between my legs.

'I've got cheese sandwiches and a pork pie in my tuck box if you want to share,' he said, tugging off the condom and slipping his still semi-erect cock away.

'Sounds great.' I jumped off the slab of metal, pulled on my knickers and straightened my uniform.

I would miss my time with Tom and his talented dick, but that was just the way it was. Cheryl would have to learn to cope with him and I'd have to find myself another well-hung pastime.

Perhaps an Italian one was in order.

Chapter Two

The plastic surgery department was set slightly apart from the general wards. It had its own gardens, a small canteen and several overnight rooms for visitors as it was a regional centre.

I was always happy to be sent there. The staff were hugely committed and experts in their field. The atmosphere was one of nurturing and support, not just for the patients but also for their families.

'Hey,' I said, strolling into the cluttered office. It was my second night on duty out of seven so I was still feeling pretty energetic. Plus last night with Tom had meant I'd had a lovely, deep, satisfying sleep all day.

'Oh, good, it's you, Sharon,' Felicity said. She was the department's head night nurse and I knew her well. We'd both been around since scalpels had been made of flint and bandages of mammoth hide.

I grinned. It was nice to be wanted. 'You busy?' I asked, grabbing a report card from the desk.

'More than usual. There's been a clinical inspection today and it knocked the late shift back several hours with everything.'

'Bummer. You want me to get on with anything straight away?'

She glanced down her chart. 'Yes, could you bedbath Ted Graham in room three? I promised I would, but I have to do the drug round first so it will be ages before I get to him.'

'No problem at all.' I glanced at his details on my sheet. Thirty-four-year-old with third degree burns to both hands. Ten days post second skin graft and reconstruction.

'Great,' Felicity said. 'But don't rush him, will you, if he wants to chat, let him. He's one of us after all.'

'He is?'

'Yep, a fireman, flames got his hands when he was rescuing a pregnant woman from a house fire.'

'Oh, damn.'

'Indeed.'

After slipping a plastic apron over my dress, I knocked quietly on the door of room three and stepped in. I shut it tight behind myself.

Ted lay on the bed, a sheet up to his waist and his head sunk into a stack of pillows. He looked big and tough with a wide chest and thick biceps, but his hands were wrapped tight in bulky white bandages, rendering him practically helpless and creating quite a contrast to the burly masculinity of his body.

He smiled when he saw me; his jawline was a wide angular shape, his teeth neat and white. Everything about him was big. He was on a whole different size scale to me.

'Hi,' I said and turned down the volume on some chat show he was watching. 'You must be Ted?'

'That's me.' His voice was deep and rasping, almost smoky. His Adam's apple bobbed as he spoke.

'I'm Sharon, would you like me to help you freshen up? Seems the day staff have been frantic.'

He rolled his eyes. 'You can say that again, they've been buzzing around like a bunch of bees that've had their nest kicked.' He laughed. 'Quite funny to sit back and watch, and not have to do anything to help. I'm used to being in the middle of all the action.'

I liked Ted already. It was the twinkle in his eye, the buoyancy of his voice. He was having a rubbish time, but when people could still smile in that state I couldn't help but admire them. I didn't know if I would, given the same situation.

'We'll keep ourselves locked out of the way,' I said, pulling a face. 'Far from the madding crowd.'

'Good plan.' He tried to sit up but struggled when a pillow slipped and he couldn't stop it falling to the floor.

I pulled his table away from the bed and adjusted his back support. Redoing his pillows.

'Sorry,' he said, 'these damn hands are not up to much at the moment.' He lifted his bandaged fists causing his pectoral muscles to flex and twitch.

I touched his warm, tendon-rich forearm and smiled gently. 'That's why I'm here, to help.'

'I haven't seen you before,' he said. 'Even though I've been laid in this room for three weeks now and going backward and forwards to theatre.'

'No, I haven't been here for about a month.'

'Ah, have you been somewhere exotic on a long, luxury holiday with a handsome doctor?'

I laughed. 'I wish.' Mmm, four weeks on a deserted island with Javier would certainly give me a boost in all departments. 'Nope, I've just been working on different wards. I'm a bit of a jack-of-all-trades, they send me wherever is low staffed at the beginning of each shift. Tonight I'm afraid you've drawn the short straw.'

'Hardly the short straw,' he said, tipping his head and studying me with a naughty glint in his eyes.

I laughed. 'Nice of you to say so. Do you want a drink?' I nodded at the empty glass on the table. It had a white straw sticking from it.

'Please, there's some Coke over there.'

I glanced at where he'd indicated. He had a small, bright red fridge humming in the corner.

'I had it delivered here from Argos.' Ted smiled. 'I

32

hate warm drinks, even in the winter. A habit from days in sunnier climates.'

'Great idea.' I opened the small glass door. 'Hey, you've got some beer in here. Want one?' I turned to him.

He looked at the closed door that led to the ward, as if seeing a frowning authority on the other side. 'Well, I don't know if I'm allowed.'

I laughed. 'Yes, you're allowed. It's your beer, you're a grown man. Have one if you want.' I picked up an icy cold can and held it aloft.

'Will you join me?'

I shook my head and widened my eyes. 'I think that might just get me fired faster than a ball out of a cannon.'

He grinned and I sensed he was swaying.

'What about the drugs I'm on?' he asked.

'No worries. It isn't strong beer, so one will be perfectly fine and it will probably help you get a good night's sleep.'

'I could sleep for the Olympics these days. Not much else to do.' He rolled his eyes and I thought his mood might switch, but then he grinned. 'Go on then, if you're sure it'll be all right.'

'I'm sure.' I shut the fridge and picked up a tall glass from a shelf. 'Have you had family in today?'

He shook his head. 'No, not today, and not tomorrow either.'

That surprised me. I would have thought his people would be swarming around him. 'Why not?'

'Just how it is for me.'

'No family?'

'Nope.' I held the glass as he took a sip of the beer through the straw. His lips were wide and plump, the bottom one held a small dink at the centre. I noticed there was a good couple of days' worth of black stubble over his cheeks, jaw and down his neck.

'Ahh, that's so good,' he said with a sigh. 'Reminds me of being in Greece; with the sun on my back, a heart full of hope and a lust for adventure.'

I walked to the sink, set about filling up a bowl of water and collecting washing paraphernalia. 'Greece. I'd love to go there.'

'Beautiful place if you can cope with wasps and earthquakes.'

'Can you tell me about it?'

'You really want to hear?'

'Yes, absolutely. I'll give you a bit of a wash while you talk. It will make me feel like I've had that holiday. I could do with one.' Plus I liked the lilt of his accent, I couldn't place it but it was light and complemented the rich throatiness of his voice.

'Couldn't we all.' He paused, then, 'I grew up in Greece. My father had a job with the government and was posted in Athens. It meant we had a nice house with a pool and a maid. Me and my sister went to a private English school but also learnt to speak fluent Greek. It's like that when you're kids. You pick up languages without even having to think about it, don't you?'

I nodded and wiped his face with the warm, soapy flannel. When I dried, the sound of stubble rasping on the towel was loud in the quiet room. 'Would you like me to give you a shave?'

He opened his eyes and looked straight into mine. They were a stunning shade of dark blue, like the deepest part of the ocean. 'Would you mind? Have you got time?'

'No, not at all, and yes I have time. It won't take long.'

'That would be great then.' He smiled again and then clicked his tongue on the roof of his mouth. 'I hate being so dependent. It's not me at all.'

'Hopefully it will only be for a few more weeks, and that's why we're here, to help.' I reached for a razor and a can of shaving foam. Flooding my hand with white froth and beginning to spread it around his jawline, the short tough hairs were sharp on my fingertips and the feeling briefly reminded me of my fun with Tom the night before.

'Well, thanks, I appreciate it, everything you all do,' he said, his mouth a dark slash in the frothy mess on his face.

'No worries.'

Silence descended upon us as I began to carefully scrape the wet razor down his right cheek. I was aware that he was watching my face intently, almost like he could see the reflection of what I was doing in my eyes. I was leaning in close, I had to, breaching personal space was the only way to perform my task, but if he looked downwards there was no doubt he'd get a flash of cleavage.

But he didn't look down, he carried on starting intently at my face and carefully twisting his mouth to stretch the skin on his cheek.

Little waves of prickles ran up my spine, nape and onto my scalp. I had a sudden sweep of self-consciousness. I was being scrutinised, closely, but I was also being trusted to wield a razor against a stranger's face and throat. It was a great privilege to be so trusted. Who was I kidding? I was hot and tingly because Ted was an incredibly handsome fireman and I was performing an intimate task for him. Donning a nurse's uniform didn't quell my appreciation for a gorgeous bloke with a sexy smile, a roguish voice and a history of saving women from burning buildings.

I straightened and jiggled the razor in the water to rid it of the stubble and used foam. 'Carry on telling me about Greece. I sense there's an "until" coming up,' I said with a smile then nibbled on my bottom lip.

He twitched his eyebrows. 'You'd be right. I was seventeen when it all started to go wrong. I had dreams of going to university in the UK and studying marketing.'

'Marketing, interesting.' With my fingertip I gently smoothed the froth beneath his nose, trying my best not to get it in his nostrils. He kept very still while I shaved around his top lip, just pulling his mouth down a little to elongate the skin.

Top lip smooth, I carried on shaving, moving around to the opposite side of his face. Still he didn't talk, he stayed silent, his breaths warm and tickly on my arm. My own breathing became slow and steady as I concentrated.

The stubble came away easily, leaving a perfect stretches of golden skin in its wake. I repeated the process over and over, sloshing the razor in the bowl of water after each downward track. Eventually I finished and dabbed his now silky jaw with the damp flannel and a warm towel. Admiring my work as opposed to the ruggedly handsome planes of his face – or so I told myself.

He touched his cheek to his hunched up shoulder, rubbed briefly, as if checking my work. 'Thanks, that's great. I can tell you've done that before.'

'A few times.' I smiled, tipped the water away and refilled the bowl. 'So did you do your marketing course?'

'Yep, I applied to several universities and was accepted into Manchester. I couldn't wait to go and start my new student life. Though to be honest, thoughts of girls were considerably more prominent than my desire to learn. Well, unless you counted my interest in studying the female form, that is.'

He laughed as I wiped the warm flannel over his broad chest. His muscles were firm and solid, neatly squared pecs and small dark nipples. Just a hint of hair over his sternum. His flesh held an olive glow, like the Greek sunshine was still within him. It was impossible not to appreciate his sturdy, sculpted physique, though I was careful not to linger with the soapy flannel. That wouldn't have been professional at all.

'And I was right,' he said as I dried with a long sweeping movements. 'The girls at uni were hot. Hot with a capital H. And willing too. Not like where I'd grown up. Back in Athens, I'd been seeing this local girl, Phedra. She had long black hair; it felt like silk and never tangled in my fingers. I found it fascinating how I could stroke right through it and it flowed like water and tickled the back of my wrists. You know, this sensitive part?' He lifted his hand, the underside of his wrist facing my way.

I nodded, gently raised his arm higher and soaped beneath it, swirling the flannel over curls of golden underarm hair. 'Was she your first love?'

He allowed me to hold his arm up. 'Phedra? Yes, I suppose she was. Hormones go a bit nuts when you're that age, don't they? I wasn't sure if I was in love with her, like as a person, or her body. She had great tits … shit, I'm sorry, Sharon.' He frowned. 'You don't want to hear this.'

'Hey, don't mind me, and of course I want to hear your story.' I towelled where I'd washed, the underarm hair fluffing as it dried. 'And believe me, there isn't anything you can say that will shock me. I've been hanging around this place too long for that.'

'I'll try and shock you then, shall I? Just for the fun of it.' He grinned.

'Go on, tell me, just for the fun of it, and I promise not to faint.' I smirked wickedly then pressed my lips together to ensure I didn't appear flirty, because that wouldn't be right at all. Not with a patient. Though I couldn't help but think it was a damn shame Ted was going to be stuck in here, out of action for a few months. We could have swapped numbers and arranged a naked rendezvous.

He matched my smile and nodded at his beer again. I held it for him as he slurped, then set it back on the table.

'Phedra, like I said, was a hottie. Her breasts were the subject of all my fantasies. Many a time I tossed off thinking what they'd feel like if I squeezed them together and put my ...' He hesitated, then shrugged, as if making a decision to just say it as it was. 'My dick between them. Warm, soft, tight. I even had a photograph of her with this itsy-bitsy bikini on. I would set it above two pillows and pretend it was really her. Not that I looked at her face, just her cleavage. Which was all well and good, this fantasy,' he said, 'until Uriana, our Greek maid, walked in to my bedroom and caught me coming all over Phedra's smiling face.' He paused. 'Am I shocking you yet?'

'No, not at all.' A bit, maybe, but by his candid honesty more than his teenage actions.

I washed his abdomen meticulously and tenderly. Thinking how much physical exercise he must have endured to get such deeply ridged muscles etched into his stomach. I suddenly became aware that I was prolonging the task and he'd stopped chatting to watch me. Quickly I reached for the towel. 'And then what?' I asked, swallowing tightly.

'It's good to be able to talk,' he said, watching me dry. 'It's like going on a trip down memory lane. I've spent too much time just sitting here thinking lately. Weird how thoughts swirl inside your head, when you have an injury that could be life changing.'

'Hopefully not "too" life changing,' I said. 'And, yes, it is good to talk, so come on, what happened when the maid walked in? You're keeping me in suspense.'

He widened his eyes and shook his head. 'Oh, yeah. Shit, I thought the roof was going lift off the villa. The sight of me, butt naked, on my knees ...' He hesitated, blew out a breath and shook his head.

I tried to rid the image he'd created in my brain. It was pretty hot, especially if I imagined him in that position as a man, and not as a teen.

'Yeah, me,' he went on, 'butt naked, on my knees, exploding over a photo of a smiling brunette. The maid screams, drops the mop and bucket of water she's carrying and runs onto the landing as though the hounds of hell are after her. Well, I'm just frozen. Time's stopped. It wasn't until I saw Phedra's face, smiling up at me and wearing some freakish pearly face-mask that I realised what was happening. I jumped up pretty sharpish then. Pulled on my clothes and spent the next ten minutes calming Uriana down and bribing her with my entire stash of drachma, this was before Euros you see. In the end, in return for payment, she promised not to say anything to my parents when they got home. There must have been the equivalent of fifty quid in my wallet, a month's wages for her, at least. Luckily she stuck to her word, though she never walked into my room again without knocking.'

'I bet she didn't.' I reached for a clean, black T-shirt from his locker, shook it and held it up. 'Do you want to wear this overnight?'

'Yeah, that will do. Got it from a U2 concert years ago.'

'Nice.' I helped him slip it on, being careful to stretch the sleeves wide over his hands and making sure there were no creases in his back. I then pulled back the sheet. He wore red boxer shorts and his long legs were thick, strong and hair-coated. There was an oblong dressing over his right thigh.

'Worst thing about the whole thing,' he said, resting his head back as I started to carefully wash his legs. 'Was it took so long for me to guarantee Uriana's silence that when I got back to Phedra's photograph, my goddamn

41

cum had wrecked it, fizzed it away or something. I was more fed up about that than Uriana walking in on me. I tried to clean it up, even had a go at drawing in her cleavage again and the outlines of her bikini top and nipples – which, by the way, you could just see straining through. There must have been a breeze on the beach that day or something.' He laughed. 'Or something. In my naivety I liked to think since I'd taken the shot that she was turned-on by me. I'd been feeling all macho and muscled up since I'd just hit six foot. I pretended, on several occasions, that she was actually thinking about us in bed together as I'd taken the picture.' He sighed. 'What happened next didn't quite go to plan, though.'

'And the plan was?'

'You sure you want to hear?'

He really was a talker, and getting quite into his story. I wiped and dried his kneecaps. 'I wouldn't be listening otherwise, I'd be making some excuse that I had other patients to see to.'

He looked worried. 'Do you?'

'No, not at all.' I smiled. 'Just you, so carry on. I'm intrigued.'

'It was a disaster,' he said, 'after my photograph of Phedra was ruined, I made a pact with myself that I wouldn't go to university without at least touching her breasts. Heck, I was seventeen, that should have been a tick on my scorecard already and so should several other things. Most of my mates were going all the way with their birds, so they'd said.

'About two weeks later I was out with Phedra. We'd been to a disco with a group of friends. She'd been glued to my side all night, touching my chest, kissing my neck. Really staking her claim on me in front of all the other girls. I could have taken my pick of them in reality. I had sun-blond hair, a tan, and as I said, I'd shot up that year.

'The disco was good. Phedra and I danced wildly. I flung her about, she laughed, I pressed her to me and she giggled and told me I was the only one for her. When a slow song came on at the end, I dragged her close, so close her soft, big breasts pressed against my chest and I swear I could feel her nipples poking at my shirt. Naturally, the snake in my trousers went from asleep to wide-awake in the space of a nanosecond, and there was nothing I could do to hide it. Part of me didn't want to, so I kept her close. Real close. Jesus, I can still remember the look on her face now. Wide eyes, a quick "oh" of surprise and then she tugged on her bottom lip with her teeth and kinda smiled. Damn, that gesture was so innocent yet so bloody erotic.'

I licked my lips and realised, with a flutter in my chest, that I'd been doing the exact same thing as I'd shaved him. Had he thought that was erotic too?

'I hope you don't think less of me for this next bit, Sharon, but remember I was a horny teenager, and I was yet to get myself any action, of any description.'

43

'Not at all. It's all part of life.'

'Yeah, you're right about that.' He paused. 'So I took her home, I always did, and when we got there, me still hard as an iron girder – God knows how I managed to walk – we noticed her parents were out. I asked if I could come in. Get a drink. It was July, hot enough to fry eggs on the road, even at night.

'Her house was small, frilly, if you know what I mean. Lace doilies, crocheted tablecloths: effigies of Christ all over the place, on the wall, on the fireplace, even on top of the fridge. We guzzled water, but then while I had thoughts of going into her bedroom and persuading her to finally show me her beautiful breasts, she opted for the sofa in the living room. Said she wanted to show me some history book of her father's or something. So I sat next to her, horny as heck, and not even trying to disguise that fact. I looked at her chest, jiggling slightly under the low-cut, polka-dot dress she wore and eventually, I took the plunge and went for a kiss that was full of passion.

'She matched my enthusiasm and my hopes soared. This was it. Phedra was as into it as I was. Her chest was mashed against mine, her nipples tight. Her tits were big but she felt so small, with tiny shoulders, delicate arms squeezing me. I felt like a man, you know, and I couldn't wait to prove that I was one.

'I lowered her down, onto her back, surprised that she was letting me take such control. She usually stopped

44

our kisses if my breaths got a bit heavy. But not this time. No, this time her breaths were as heavy as mine, her little hands were skimming up and down my body. I spread kisses down her neck – her skin tasted of vanilla and sherbet, kind of summery but also dead sexy.

'I was growing bolder, exploring the first rise of her breasts with my tongue. She slid her hands into my hair, arched her back, pressing herself into me. Encouraged, I slipped the straps of her dress from her shoulders and exposed her gorgeous chest. She didn't wear a bra so my access was unhindered and I had none of the agonised fumbling my mates complained of when trying to undo clips and catches, know what I mean?'

I nodded.

'She was perfect and fitted in my hand just right. I can still remember the weight of the outside slopes as I squashed them together, creating that channel my horny teenage imagination had been dreaming about for so long. She panted my name and I suckled her nipples. The most lovely gasps and sighs came from her. I was flying high. I was onto a winner. Sucking Phedra's perfect breasts was a top fantasy and fulfilling it was spinning me high. Well, it did for a few minutes, and then the damn anaconda between my legs demanded attention. I sat up. It pained me to move even an inch from her, and I was scared that I might break the spell. But luckily it didn't. She just stared at my groin, all big eyes and slack mouth as I tugged out my erection. I had to touch it carefully, I was so close to coming. One wrong move, a frantic jerk or an over-zealous squeeze and it would be all over.

'I repositioned with my legs either side of her chest. It was a bit awkward on the sofa, but I managed. She just lay there and eyed my engorged manhood like it might bite her. I said a few words of encouragement as I angled the head between her tits, and this seemed to spur her on. She squeezed the flesh together, creating that perfect tunnel between them, just what I'd fantasied about. I remember sucking in a breath, holding it deep, and then sliding through her sweat-damp cleavage. If felt amazing. Not least because she groaned like she actually enjoyed it. That hadn't been something I'd counted on. By the time I'd repeated the action my balls were tight into my body. I was so close.

'She was watching the tip of me pop out of her cleavage on each ride. I thought about sliding into her gasping mouth but decided to save that for another time. I was too close to shooting my load. I wouldn't get there.

'And then, I had my first spurting session with a real, live girl. Jizz flew from my slit, slapping onto her throat, her chin. I shunted into her breasts, fascinated by the sight of my semen landing around her mouth, her cheeks. Damn, I was proud of the serious quantities my balls could produce. She looked shocked to be honest, shocked and stunned.

'Well, I had about three seconds of being on top of the world, and thinking this was it, from now on we'd forget about discos or lounging at the beach. We had found a new pastime for whenever we hung out. Damn, she even looked like the photograph I'd jizzed over. And then the overhead light went on, brilliant and white, and her parents looked in from the living room doorway.'

'Bloody hell,' I said. 'You really didn't get much privacy as a teenager did you.'

'Tell me about it,' he groaned. 'Again I just froze and stared down at Phedra, who was sticky and gooey, and looking like someone who'd just woken up and found themselves dropped into a porn movie.

'The mother squealed and begged the Lord to save them from my hideous urges then fled to the kitchen. Her father, in Greek, told me to get my pants up. Naturally, I did, pretty sharpish, didn't want him messing with Mr Cobra down there. Phedra grabbed a red-and-white lacy shawl from the arm of the sofa, wiped her face, kind of – she missed a blob of cum just to the left of her mouth – then quickly dragged up the straps of her dress.

'It's then it becomes really shameful, if you can imagine it being more so. I told the biggest lie of my life. Her father, although a small man, managed to look like a damn ninja in that moment, and he asked me what my intentions were with his daughter. I looked to Phedra for support, but her face had drained of colour, her hands were shaking, she looked too shocked to even cry. I glanced around the room and my attention fell on a grainy photograph of Phedra's parents in a silver frame. That's when the lie came to me. I took Phedra's hand, squeezed it tight and told him that my intention was to marry his daughter.

'He still didn't look too happy, though he did unclench his fists. So I kissed Phedra's knuckles, dropped to my knee and looked into her eyes with as much sincerity as I could muster given the circumstances. I proposed then, and it felt kind of right. She let out a little sob, that blob of cum on her face wobbled, and then she nodded.

'And that was how I became engaged, the first time, at least. Her mother came running into the room and hugged me, the father shook my hand, and Phedra finally stopped shaking and I managed to discreetly wipe the last of my excitement from her face.'

'The first time?' I asked, freshening up the water and spotting a tube of aqueous cream on the shelf. 'Tell me about the second.' I set about massaging the cream into his freshly washed feet. His toes were long, the arches deep, there were a few pale hairs on his two biggest toes. He didn't react to my extra measures at preventing bedsores so I guessed he wasn't ticklish.

'I bought Phedra a ring, then much to her surprise informed her I was still going to Manchester to study. I told her this would mean a better life for us in the future. She cried to start with but eventually she saw my reasoning. Perhaps I wouldn't have gone if Phedra had let me go all the way, but she'd barely let me touch her since I'd slipped a ring on her finger.

'The thing was though, her look-but-don't-touch plan backfired. I'd barely been in Manchester a week and I was in bed with Stella, a red-haired student on my marketing course. She was as in to it as much as me, and wonderfully experienced. She used to do this rotating thing with her hips and then squeeze her internal muscles. Damn, it drove me to the edge every time. God knows how we managed to get any studying done that first term, we were insatiable.

'Did I miss Phedra? No, not a jot. I wouldn't have admitted that even to myself back then, though, I liked to pretend I wasn't that much of a scumbag. I even tried to justify it in my head that I was refining my technique ready for our wedding night. But really, I don't know who I was trying to kid. I loved being with Stella. She was hot, naughty, and just like a bloke the way she wanted to get naked anywhere, anytime, anyhow.'

'Sounds fun.'

'It was, and after Stella it was Nancy, then Emily, and then a bunch of girls whose names all kind of merge into one in my memory. I was on a frenzy for the whole three years I studied. It helped being compared to Brad Pitt who was just making a name for himself as an on-screen god back then. Personally, I thought the resemblance was tenuous, but I wasn't going to deny girls their fantasy and did my best to make them squeal in delight until the early hours of the morning.

'I never saw Phedra again. And I'm ashamed to admit that. Not to break off the engagement nor to explain myself. I just didn't go home in the holidays. My parents were shocked by my long absence from Greece and even came to see me after eighteen months with reports of Phedra's distress and her family's growing concerns for my commitment to her. I told them nothing had changed and I just wanted to be standing on my own two feet financially before taking on the responsibility of a wife.

'They left after three days, not entirely convinced and seemingly suspicious of all the pretty girls who called "hello" to me around the campus. I never saw them again, my parents. And that last meeting, that was full of deception, pains me even all these years later. They were killed the next spring, in a plane crash. They were on one of these light aircrafts and it crashed into the sea in a storm. My parents and three of my father's work colleagues and their wives were all reported missing. They'd been to Cephalonia on some work-jolly, wine-tasting weekend. It seemed the pilot had also indulged, so the inquest said.

'The bodies were never found, so no funeral as such. They had a service, of course, but I didn't go. My sister

50

never forgave me for that, and I've never forgiven myself for it either. But the thought of seeing Phedra and her parents was just too terrifying. Why, I don't know. I should have manned up and told her the situation, but while the authorities were searching for the plane for two months I fell into a place where only alcohol and shagging seemed to make the pain bearable.

'My university course came to an end. I had a degree, plenty of inherited cash and had taken to fluttering on the horses, which just added to my list of vices – women, booze and gambling. I had a big win, on a horse at Cheltenham, and decided to use the cash to do some travelling. I hopped on a plane to Vegas, the city of lights and dreams. It turned out to be a one-way ticket for several years.

'On my very first night there I met Cleo. She was tall, blonde, bubbly and from Texas. Her Southern drawl made my groin ache right from the first time she said "Howdy, cowboy, how ya doin'?" I bought her a drink and she sat with me at a roulette table in Caesars Palace. When she kissed my cheek and wished me luck right before a thousand-buck win came in, I was smitten.

'Cleo became my world. I gambled a small fortune but won a larger one. My luck just kept on growing and for six months I didn't need to work at all. Then a friend I'd made said he was opening his own casino, just off the strip. Not quite as salubrious as Vegas' other signature hotels, but classy enough for me to want to invest. With inheritance and big wins I threw up fifty per cent of the cash he needed and signed the deal on the same night I proposed for the second time in my life.

'Cleo, in her true spirit, yeha'd and leapt on me. I adored her enthusiasm for life, her ditzy nature and the fact that in her eyes I could do no wrong, despite my failings. None of which I'd ever tried to hide; she knew it all. I'd cocked up with my family, drank and gambled, but she still loved me. It made me love her all the more.

'We married, but we didn't settle in Texas, we bought a pad in Vegas. Cleo didn't need to work. She had her nails done, went to the gym, wished me luck when I threw dice. She was there for me, I was there for her, and the casino I'd invested in was making me a good living with minimal effort required. We were on a permanent holiday and for several blissful years I was happier than I thought it possible to be. 'Then Cleo began to withdraw and eventually confessed she hadn't been taking her pill and couldn't understand why she wasn't pregnant. Technically she should have been – we were at it every opportunity we got. We were like a couple of rabbits on speed. And why not, she had a body made for fantasies and was up for anything, if you know what I mean.'

'Mmm,' I said, thinking what a lucky girl this Cleo was to be rolling not just a dice but also between the sheets with Ted.

'I paid for us to go and see the best doctor in town. A ton of tests later, we got our answer. I was shooting blanks, no swimmers at all. Not one little bugger to even have a go at wriggling into an ovum. All that time I'd been so proud of my huge quantities of jizz, presuming it to be laden with tadpoles, and it was just empty juice – vodka and lemonade without the damn vodka.'

'That's bad luck,' I said. 'I'm really sorry.'

'Yeah, we were too, devastated in fact, and I began to drink heavily again, something I'd stopped doing. My luck took a downward turn at the tables, not that it mattered. I only gambled with my spare change really. The casino was my steady wage and paid the bills. I guess I was depressed again but didn't recognise it at the time.

'It was a few months before I noticed there was something different about Cleo. She was putting on weight, eating weird stuff and sleeping all the time. She couldn't hide her pregnancy from me for another day.

'Her confirmation of my suspicion really turned my world upside down. That feeling, dreams coming true, existed for an entire three seconds, then she blurted out that the baby was Stan's. Stan was my best friend, the guy I'd set up the casino with. It seemed during my depression Stan had been cheering Cleo up, not with a box of chocolates and a bunch of flowers, but with his big, fat, cheating dick.

'If I thought I'd been depressed before, then now I

was rock bottom. Cleo announced that she was in love with Stan and wanted to divorce me and marry him so he could raise his child. Talk about getting kicked in the guts when you're already down. I'm pretty sure I would have made a go of it, with her and the baby, if she'd just given me some time to get used to the idea. I loved her with all my heart and could have loved her child. But Cleo always was an instant gratification kind of girl. If she wanted something she wanted it now, and right then, she wanted Stan.

'So there was nothing left for me to do but sell the house and move away. I didn't fancy Greece and a sister who still wouldn't speak to me and a fiancée who I hoped had moved on with her life but would probably still garrote me given the chance.'

'So that's how you came back to the UK?' I asked, finishing up with his feet and putting the cream back on the shelf.

'Yes, I went to Manchester. It was where I knew and I took a job in marketing. I hated it, despite climbing the ranks pretty quickly. Everyone there was such a shark, ready to take chunks out of one another to look good or claim an idea or strategy. I might not be a model citizen, but I knew right from wrong, and the things that went on at this place, well it was just plain immoral.

'So five years ago, divorced, alone, and in a job I hated, I upped sticks to the Dales and joined the fire

54

service. It wasn't as well paid as marketing. But for the first time I felt like I was doing something worthwhile. The guys I worked with were salt-of-the-earth types and the people I helped genuinely in need. I finally found a sense of peace within myself.'

He sighed, and I helped him drink a little more of his beer. He gulped quickly, taking over half the drink in one go.

'Until three weeks ago,' he said licking his lips. 'That damn beam came down and this happened.' He held up his bandaged hands. 'I guess it could have been worse though.'

'Yep, you could not be here at all, same goes for the person you saved,' I said, squeezing out the flannel.

He gave a small shudder. 'I know, I'm used to risking myself but the thought of a bad judgment or a twist of fate having implications for someone else makes my blood run cold if I think about it too much.'

'I know what you mean.'

'Yeah, I'm sure, doing the job you do.'

Our eyes connected briefly.

'So have you been going through all of this alone?' I asked.

'I've got good friends, the best. The guys from the station have been in and out visiting.' He sighed. 'But an accident like this, it kind of reminds them all of their own mortality and the risks they take on a daily basis. It's not easy viewing.'

'What about your sister? Has she been to see you?'

'No. I sent her a letter two weeks ago. I know it arrived in Greece, I sent it recorded delivery. She signed for it but she hasn't answered. Not yet anyway.'

I shook my head. What a cow. An injured brother and she ignores him because of something that happened years ago. Life was too short. I had no siblings and would have done just about anything to have a brother or sister when I was growing up. Some people didn't know how lucky they were.

'Hey, don't look sorry for me,' he said. 'That's the last thing I need. I'm sure it will all work out.' He grinned. 'Me and Mr Cobra down there have had some serious fun, and one thing I've learnt is you've gotta take the ups with the downs. This is just one of the downs, I'll get through it no matter what the future holds.' His eyes sparkled, telling his story had obviously made him wonder what direction his life would take from here. Would he be able to go back to the job that had finally given him his place in the world and brought him peace?

'Of course you'll be fine. These injuries can heal amazingly despite what they first look like plus you're getting the best possible treatment here.' I smiled and nodded at his groin. 'And part of that treatment means, I'm afraid, it's time to wash Mr Cobra if that's okay?'

He shrugged and a rise of colour bloomed on his cheeks. He averted his eyes from mine. 'Sure thing.'

I pulled his boxers down, exposing his cock, then carefully washed him. When I'd finished I reached for the towel and set about the job of drying.

I glanced up.

He'd dropped his head back onto the pillow. His lips were a tight, flat line and his bandaged hands rested on the bed at his side. His breaths were coming a little fast. The red bloom on his cheeks had deepened.

I carried on drying. I'd washed and dried thousands of cocks, big and small, long and short. It was just part of my job. Nothing to get worked up about. Nothing to be embarrassed about.

He blew out a slow breath, the air breezing over my arm.

I glanced up at him again, and then noticed, with shock, that there was a stiffening in his penis.

He lifted his head and squirmed. 'Shit, sorry. Sharon, fucking hell ...' He wore an expression of acute mortification, tugging on his bottom lip with his teeth and his eyes narrowed to thin slits.

'It's OK,' I said. I hadn't quite finished drying. 'Natural reaction to stimulation.'

'Well, you better stop stimulating.' He swallowed tightly. 'Or my problem here is just going to get worse.'

I dried his cock a little firmer, in a movement that I knew would elicit a groan. I couldn't help it. Something just took over me. I had to do it.

'Ah, ah …' he gasped and his abdominal muscles tensed. 'That feels nice but it's gotta be way out of your job description.'

'What, helping an injured man feel a little more … comfortable?' Damn, what was the matter with me? My hands were acting of their own accord, a devil inside me was prodding my arms with his shocking little fork and shouting 'go on, go on'.

'Comfortable is one way of putting it.' Ted sucked in a deep breath, his wide chest expanding and his teeth gritting. His gaze was fixed on his groin.

'You want me to stop?' I asked. I had the towel spread out and was holding his shaft over the top of it. I could have got away with saying I was still drying it, but barely – my movements were recognisable as stimulating to any adult across the four corners of the world.

'I feel I should say yes, stop. Morally, that is,' he said in a tense voice. 'But …'

The head of his cock was poking out of the towel and protruding from his foreskin. He was heading to full hardness pretty quickly and I couldn't help but be impressed that Mr Viper, or whatever he'd called it, was in such good form after all he'd been through recently. 'But what, Ted?'

'But, fuck, all that talking about shagging, a cold beer and then you doing that. I couldn't help it.'

'You want me to carry on?' I could get into so much

shit for this. I knew that. But sod it. Ted deserved to be treated like a man, the hero he was. And, at the end of the day, with those bandaged hands he could hardly bring himself any relief. This was a mercy mission and I was the only one here to stand up for the job.

'Ted? Do you want me to carry on,' I asked again.

'Yes,' he said almost in a whisper. His gaze caught mine. 'If you don't mind.'

'I don't mind at all.' And I suddenly realised I didn't. What was the definition of holistic care? Attending to all of your patients needs. Well, I was just taking that one step further. Maslow would be proud of the lengths I was going to help Ted reach self-actualisation. Well, self-actualising for a few minutes, at least.

'Jesus fucking Christ,' he groaned, staring down at my hand, which I was working faster now. 'The only thing I've felt for weeks is pain, so that is ... what you're doing is ...'

'Good?'

'Yeah.' A small shudder rippled up his body. 'Good is one way to describe it.'

Now I was convinced. If there had been any pretence that I wasn't wanking him off it went out of the window. I ditched the towel and gripped his cock. He was a well-hung guy and hefty in my fist, and I began a firm push-pull motion, the last of the moisture from the flannel sliding my grip.

'Ah, yeah,' he said, breathlessly. 'That time when I came on Phedra. It was so wrong but so damn good. A bit like this. Thank you, Sharon.'

'Shh, no talking.' I glanced at the door.

He closed his eyes, pursed his lips. His strong hips jolted, as though thrusting for more of my touch. The headboard rattled against the wall.

I got into my task. His cock bloated further, the slit strained open. His pulse was hard against my palm. I shot a look at the door again, praying no one would come in.

'Ah, ah,' he panted. 'Fuck, yeah. That's it.'

Jesus, I'd be super impressed if he came this quickly but it would certainly be a good thing, given the illicit, high-risk nature of my actions.

I upped the pace, squeezed a little tighter. My heart was thumping so hard I could hear the pulse in my ears. Then with a throaty groan he came. Cum spurted from his slit onto the clean U2 T-shirt. He hadn't been lying when he'd said he could produce cupfuls. On and on it burst from him. I kept working, eking out every last drip like it was some kind of tap I was draining.

The deep moans erupting from him vibrated throughout his body. His back arched, his head pressed into the pillow. His body was alive and strong and racked with toe-curling pleasure. Seeing him like that was glorious even though it was completely wrong in a hospital bed. I couldn't help the flush of satisfaction that burst in my chest.

'Ah, yeah, oh, fuck …' he said, a deep, appreciative groan gurgling up from his chest and his spine softening against the pillows. 'That was amazing.'

'What the – what the devil is going on in here?' Another voice penetrated the room, spearing into our moment and popping the erotic bubble.

Shit! My heart stuttered. I spun to the door, still gripping Ted's throbbing cock.

Iceberg was staring at me, eyes wide as she absorbed the sackable scene she'd stumbled in on. Her lips pursed and she shut the door with a quiet click.

My stomach somersaulted then cartwheeled then did a couple of double twists just for the fun of it. Bugger!

'Oh, bloody hell,' Ted gasped. 'I know … I should feel terrible but that was the best I've felt in weeks.'

'Of course you shouldn't feel terrible,' I said in a much calmer voice than I felt. Damn. I was in so much trouble.

'But, won't you … get into … trouble?' He was panting like he'd run up several flights of stairs.

I released him and rested my hand on his arm. 'No, she's cool. We're best friends and we both know there's no harm in bending the rules occasionally.'

'Really?' He glanced down at the sticky mess he'd made.

'Yeah, really.' I grinned. 'I hope you have another clean T-shirt.'

He nodded and I reached into the locker. Pulled out a red Nike top.

'Sharon,' he said, holding up his bandaged hands. 'A beer and a wank for a helpless man, you're the best nurse in the world ... don't you ever forget that, no matter what.'

Chapter Three

'I don't even need to ask you to explain, Staff Nurse Roane.' Iceberg's lips pursed so tight they reminded me of a cat's bottom. I had no idea how she was actually managing to speak with her mouth like that. 'A picture,' she went on, 'paints a thousand words.' She folded her arms over her ample chest and glared at me. Cold, hard, mean eyes that didn't blink.

I squirmed on the plastic seat in her grim second-floor office and stared over her right shoulder at a grey filing cabinet topped with a dying potted plant. Poor thing, it could do with some water and some sunshine, it looked tropical. But it wouldn't last long in here, not with the arctic vibes that were being flung about.

'Surely you must realise the position you've put me in,' she said. 'Sexual liaison's with patients is completely forbidden. It's not just unprofessional it's a dismissible offence. Your job is in the balance here, you know. This could be the last time you set foot in this hospital, ever.'

Oh bloody hell.

'And when your union hears about this you can kiss goodbye to any rep support. It's hardly something they're going to be jumping up and down to defend you for. The opposite will happen. They'll kick you out faster than you can say "malignant hypertension" and that will be the end of your nursing career as well as your monthly wage packet.'

Fuck.

'And as for the Nursing and Midwifery Council.' She grinned, but not in a nice way, more in a mad Doctor Evil kind of way. 'You'll be stripped of your registration and no one will employ you without that, you're illegal then, qualified but not recognised.' She shook her head and pursed her lips into a cat's arsehole again.

I hung my head, knotted my fingers in my lap and fought the moisture welling in my eyes. I would not let the evil bitch see me cry. No way. Even if I lost everything. I would not let her see I was upset about it.

'And in a regional plastic surgery unit too.' She stood and paced around her desk towards me. Her footsteps were heavy on the wiry carpet and her bulk created a draught on my bare arm as she walked past.

I got the impression that in her head she was acting out a scene from some cop drama. Pretending to be the super-clever detective that had cracked a case and now just had to get her suspect to squeal. That ridiculous thought helped stave off the tears. I bit my lip and sucked in a deep breath.

'Jesus Christ,' she said, standing behind me, bending and talking into my ear. 'A helpless, defenceless man who can do nothing for himself!'

I forced myself not to jerk away. Not to show weakness. Any crack and she would turn it into a crevasse.

'What the hell were you thinking? Seriously, staff nurse, tell me.'

I kind of shrugged, sort of. There was no denying what she'd seen, but what I'd been thinking, well, that was a different matter. She saw Ted as a man who now relied on others from the minute he woke to the moment he went to sleep. But, of course, that hadn't always been the case and after hearing his life story I felt I knew him. He'd loved and lost, had his ups and downs, he'd made mistakes and tried to fix them, but ultimately he was a fine and brave hero. He was also a man, a man with needs, one of them I'd been able to fulfil and make him happy on an evening where he would otherwise be staring at the TV immersed in worries for the future and trying to ignore the pain in his hands.

'You were masturbating a patient,' Iceberg said in a slow and deliberate voice, drawing out the word 'masturbating' into four long syllables. 'Masturbating a sick, vulnerable patient when you were supposed to be caring for him. Helping him wash.' She moved around to the side, rested her knuckles on the table, and stared at me.

Now I knew she was pretending to be DC Iceberg. If she could have had a set of cuffs hanging on her belt next to the massive set of keys that swung there, I'm pretty sure she would have.

What the hell does Javier see in her? Power-crazy cow.

I gulped and willed myself to think of a solution to this enormous pile of crap I'd managed to land myself in.

Lose my job. Lose my registration. That couldn't happen. Since Michael had left two years ago I had a mortgage to pay on my own, a loan that required monthly deposits, not to mention the holiday to Ibiza that I was still paying off from last year.

Damn. I needed the money like I needed to breathe. I could end up bankrupt just from doing a good deed? And I would if Iceberg got her way.

'It was what you saw,' I said, trying to hide the wobble in my voice. If she thought I was feeble she'd go for the jugular even quicker. 'But not for the reasons you think. There's no kind of relationship between us other than a professional one.'

She straightened, folded her arms again and looked down her nose at me. 'Go on.'

'He's a young guy and had a really terrible time lately after risking his life to save a pregnant woman, so let's be honest about his needs.'

'Honesty would be refreshing in this place.' She moved

66

back to her seat, sat and curled her fingers around the lip of the table in front of her. 'Tell me more about these "needs".'

'I'd helped him wash, as you said, and he'd told me all about his wife and how she'd run off with his best friend when he found out he couldn't have children. He'd lost his parents in a plane crash and his sister disowned him. He's now a fireman and spends his days putting himself in danger to rescue others.'

She clicked her tongue. 'So you thought you'd cheer him up?'

'Well yes, kind of, but it just happened. It wasn't exactly planned. He got a stiffy, er, I mean an erection when I was washing him. It happens, doesn't it? You must know.'

She neither shook nor nodded her head, just glared.

I steeled myself to stay strong. 'And then suddenly, he was groaning and not in pain, but with pleasure. I stopped straight away, I was drying him then, and I was, naturally, completely shocked. So was he, but even so he asked me to go on. Well, I knew it was wrong, but ...' I leant forward, trying to appeal to any dormant scrap of humanity in her. 'But how could I refuse a man who has no function with his hands? I just couldn't. Not when I could tell it would only be a quick couple of strokes and then all over.'

She raised her eyebrows.

'It was very wrong of me to go through with what he wanted, and I'll apologise to you and the hospital profusely, if that's what you need me to do, but ...' I paused. 'I don't regret what I did. That man had probably the first genuine smile on his face and the first snippet of pleasure rather than agony from his body in weeks. He needed that more than I needed to be professional.'

I folded my arms, held her gaze and raised my chin a little. What I'd said was true. I would regret losing my job – damn, that would land me up shit creek without a paddle – but would I regret making Ted come? No, that would never be a regret of mine. I would always believe I'd made the right decision on that one. I had to; it was the only way to stay sane.

'Mmm,' she said, rubbing her chin. 'I see.'

A small flicker of hope swirled in my chest. Quickly I squashed it down. Iceberg was known for her lack of compassion. She wouldn't understand Ted's needs nor believe my story. Who was I kidding? I was done for. I may as well hang myself now.

The tears threatened again, but like last time, I blinked them away, willing them to reabsorb into my eyeballs. Don't cry, don't cry, I repeated in my mind.

Eventually she broke the silence. 'Did you tell any of the department nurses why you had to leave and come immediately to my office?'

'No, I just got my bag and left.'

'So the only people who know about this incident are you, me and Mr Graham?'

'Yes.' That flicker was trying to ignite again. What the hell was she getting at?

'Mmm, that is one good thing I suppose.'

My mouth was dry, and my heart romped up another notch. Really? She wasn't going to have me flogged by a group of whip-wielding, paper-pushing personnel types who took delight in beating the real workers?

She breathed deep, narrowed her eyes, and tugged on her bottom lip. 'Perhaps this could stay between us.'

OK, so now there was a real, live flame of hope burning in my guts. This maybe wasn't the end of my nursing career, a roof over my head, and food on the table!

She tapped the tips of her fingers together. 'No, no, I'm sorry that won't work.'

'Yes it will.'

'What if he tells his family when they visit?'

'He doesn't have any family. He's all alone in the world. Just a few work colleagues and that's it.'

She continued to tap her fingers. 'Are you sure?'

'Yes.'

'Because this will be my neck on the line, too, you know, if I don't report it.'

'I understand that, and I appreciate that you'd keep this under wraps for me. I really can't afford to lose my job, and certainly not my registration. Nursing is all I know. It's my life, I can't do anything else.'

'Well, I think tonight you proved there'll always be an alternative career for you, Nurse Roane.'

Bitch. I rolled my lips in on themselves, held the word back. It was hard, it sat big and heavy on my tongue. Tickling my throat and catching my breaths, it wanted to come out into the open so badly.

She gave a gruff laugh. 'Yeah, I know, everyone hates me. But I don't care. It's not my job to be popular. I'm paid to keep this place running smoothly and make sure the patients are well cared for and happy.'

Some nurses can do that and still be nice people. But I didn't say that either. I was dangling by a thread, my situation as precarious as it could be.

'So,' she said, 'how would it suit you if we just draw a line under the whole incident and forget it ever happened?'

'That would be great. And I promise it will never happen again. Never, nothing like it at all.' I was sweating now, despite the cool room. My underarms were damp and I could feel moisture on my brow. 'I promise.'

'Good. In that case, we'll turn a blind eye to your blatant disregard for nursing ethics, hospital, union and professional body protocols as well as personal morality.'

There was nothing wrong with my personal morals. The other stuff, well yes, that was all true, but morally, I felt I'd been in the right, damn it. 'Great. Thanks.' I stood, desperate to get out of there and away from her weird and uncharacteristically kind gesture.

'Wait, not so fast,' she said. 'Sit down.'

I did as she asked. My heart, which had been soaring, was now sinking. I knew it had been too good to be true.

'Whilst I appreciate your words of thanks, a return gesture is in order.'

'I don't know what you mean?' Yeah, I did. I should have guessed she'd want something for letting me off. The words deal and devil came to mind.

'I have a little problem, you see. Well, actually it's not so little. It's a big old pain in the arse problem that I'm getting sat on for.'

I raised my eyebrows.

'You might be the perfect person to help me out,' she said, tipping her head and studying me.

'I will if I can.'

'Oh, you will, yes, you most definitely will.' She pursed her lips again, and I forced myself to look at the withering plant rather than her cat-bum mouth.

'You go to just about every ward in the hospital during the course of a month or so, don't you?' she said.

'Yes, I suppose.'

'So you know everyone, and I don't just mean nurses, but doctors, porters, pharmacy staff, you get my drift?'

'Well, only the night shifters. I haven't worked a day shift in nearly five years. It doesn't suit me.'

'Mmm, well that's OK. Because it's something on the night shift that I need you to look into for me.'

I had to admit, I was a little intrigued. Iceberg had a problem that her superiors were getting agitated about. She needed my help so badly she was prepared to let me off a massive misdemeanour instead of sitting back and enjoying watching me getting professionally hung, drawn and quartered. 'What's that then?' I asked.

'This will stay between us, won't it?'

'Yes, I'm not going to risk you telling Personnel about my little slip from protocol, am I?'

'No, I suppose not, but what I mean is, I don't want whoever is doing it tipped off that I'm onto him or her.'

Tipped off? 'Why, what is it?'

'Someone.' She leant forward and narrowed her eyes, 'is taking benzodiazepines from pharmacy. Out of the night stock cupboard.'

'Bloody hell, really?' OK, now that had my attention. Some arsehole was taking drugs for recreational use, from my hospital. That wasn't on. That shit was for patients. 'What's going missing?'

'Temazepam. Quite a bit of it too. It has to be signed for, so we know just how much there's supposed to be in the emergency cupboard, but every week or so, I go and it's just about cleared out.'

'And you have no idea who's doing it?'

'Nope. No idea at all.' She lifted her huge silver clunk

of keys and jiggled them. 'I'm the only one with access to the night stock cupboard. If a ward runs out of something, they call me and I go and get it for them. But it seems that I'm no longer the only one with a key.'

'Maybe it's someone on the day staff coming back in at night?'

'I thought that too, but Personnel questioned everyone when the last lot went missing. All eighteen staff with key access had solid alibis. So that ruled them out. It has to be someone who is a night-time regular. Could be a nurse, a porter, or even a radiographer. Who knows?'

'But how do you think I'll be able to find anything out?' If Personnel couldn't and neither could pharmacies own staff, I didn't stand a chance. I'd never even been in the emergency night drug cupboard for anything. Hadn't ever needed to.

'Because, Sharon, you know everyone and work everywhere. You slip through the wards and departments pretty much unseen, so I want you to listen to conversations, pick up on any odd behaviour or rumours and report back to me. No one really takes any notice of bank nurses, you're just there to earn your cash then go home. Likelihood is tongues will loosen if it's just you around.'

Charming. Was I really so invisible?

'So from now on ...' She sat forward, picked up a pen and pointed the nib at me. 'You're my grass, OK? Anything you hear out of the ordinary, you come and report to me. At the end of each shift I expect to see you here. Doesn't matter if you don't think it has anything to do with the missing benzos, I want to hear it. How else can I put together the puzzle if I don't have all the pieces?'

My head was spinning. 'But what if I don't hear or notice anything? What if I can't find out who's helping themselves to drugs?'

'You will, oh, you will. And what's more you have two weeks exactly to do it in. Because if you don't, then I'll be picking up that.' Using the pen she pointed at the phone on the desk. 'And calling Personnel to tell them all about your indecent misconduct with Mr Graham. And don't think it'll be my word against yours and there'll be no case if he doesn't admit to it, because it doesn't work like that. I'm senior, much more senior to you. They'll believe me, end of story.'

A knot grew in my belly. She had me by the short and curlies that was for sure. What could I do?

Nothing except play along and be her snitch.

'And you won't say a word about this little conversation to anyone, not a soul, OK,' she added.

I nodded and stood, my eyes stinging. A tightness was growing in my chest that I knew would soon turn into a sob. The relief of being let off my crime had been quickly replaced with the repulsion of being Iceberg's bitch.

She gave a twisted smile and flicked her hand towards the door.

Hurriedly I left the office. It was like the weight of the whole hospital was on my shoulders. I hated Iceberg, had done for years, and now I had to feed her information about my co-workers. If they ever found out about this I'd not just be a laughing stock but also sneered at and avoided. People would clamp their mouths shut when they saw me coming. Life would be miserable, unbearable. I'd be better off being contaminated with a superbug.

Perhaps I should face the music and own up to Personnel about my serious wander from appropriate nursing practice. At least that way I'd go down for a crime I believed in.

No. That wasn't a viable option, not financially, at least. I had to try to keep my job for the sake of my bank balance and loan repayments. My salary was not on par with a whizz-kid stockbroker, but it just about cleared the bills and fed me each month. Living without it, heading down to Tesco for a job on the tills wasn't something I could consider. Would they employ me anyway after I'd given a handjob to a helpless man?

I wandered down the quiet fire escape staircase, feeling full of doom and gloom, and headed onto one of the back corridors that led past the operating theatres. Eventually this way would send me outside so I could get back to the hospice.

The corridor was empty and lit only with dim, amber night lights. The place was still and silent, my soft-soled shoes barely disturbing the peace that was so opposite to the frenetic activity of the daylight hours. I was lost in tangled thoughts about my situation. My guts twisting with anger at Iceberg. Out of everyone here, why did it have to be her to walk into that room? Why did anyone have to at all?

Suddenly I was grabbed from behind. A big hand slapped over my mouth and I was dragged backwards against a long, lean body. To my horror I was manoeuvred through a doorway into a store cupboard, my feet tripping over themselves, my torso held tight.

'Mmmm ...' I huffed, my voice muffled against a warm, smooth palm. I went to twist, tried to scream. Panic raged in my ears and blasted into my veins.

'Shh, Sharon, it's only me, be quiet.'

Fuck, really?

'Carl!' I squeaked.

He removed his hand. 'Shh, I want to show you something.'

I turned within his arms and slapped my fists against his chest. My right one hit the hard end of his stethoscope and I winced. 'You really scared me, you dickhead. What the bloody hell do you –?'

'Shh.' He grinned down at me. Behind his glasses the whites of his eyes sparkled in the shadowy light and his hair flopped messily around his face. 'It will be worth it, I promise.'

I frowned in bitter annoyance, but even as I did a surge

of relief welled within me that it was only Carl who'd grabbed me. God only knew some weird things went on around here, and the kind of night I was having, well, it could have just gone from really fucking bad, to truly horrific had it been a drunk from casualty with a nurse fetish or an escapee from the acute psych ward who had a grudge against anyone in uniform. A shudder rattled up my spine at the thought.

'Hey,' he whispered, tilting my chin with his thumb. 'Sorry, I really didn't mean to scare you so badly.'

'Well you did, you prick.' The tears that had been so efficiently reabsorbed when I'd been in Iceberg's office sprang forth. 'I didn't know it was you, did I? It could have been a right nutter –' I gulped down a sob.

'Bloody hell, Sharon, I'm so sorry. I thought you'd laugh.'

He pulled me close and I buried my face in the crook of his neck. I was more than happy to be held after the unpleasant encounter I'd just had with Iceberg.

Carl smelled of the slightly citrusy aftershave he always wore, though it was faded and tinged with the scent of male and an unfamiliar washing detergent. I squeezed my eyes shut and gave up to the inevitability of several tears and allowed them to roll fatly down my cheeks and onto his white coat. I tried to hold a sob in but my chest still heaved, the air broke free, and I did a weird juddering thing with my shoulders.

'Shh,' he soothed, stroking my hair. 'Shh, don't cry. God, I'm such an idiot.'

'Yes, you are, but it's not just that you scared me,' I managed against his neck, my nose brushing the scratchy stubble that grew beside his Adam's apple. 'I've just had a really awful night, that's all.'

'Wanna talk about it?' he asked, his mouth pressing into my temple, his breath warm in my hair.

Yes!

I shook my head. 'No.' I tightened my arms around his waist and was rewarded by an even firmer return hug. He breathed deep, like he was smelling my hair, then slid his hand into the small of my back and rubbed the little pain that was often there as if he knew it existed.

Luckily the tears were short-lived. I put it down to being held by Carl. I'd fancied him for ages and had done nothing about it. But now, feeling that, although slim, he actually had some damn fine muscles going on beneath his clothes – long and sinewy with a definite, concrete strength to them – I began to wonder why I'd lingered. Being in his arms was nice. More than nice, it felt lovely.

'You OK?' he whispered, shifting so he could look down at me.

'Yes.' I nodded and wiped my cheek.

'I really am sorry. I promise I won't ever grab you from behind again.'

I rolled my eyes. 'Oh yeah?'

'Well, maybe I won't promise.' His sudden grin made me think he'd been imagining us naked together, the way I had. 'And,' he said, 'if you change your mind and want a friend to talk to, then just holler, OK?'

'Thanks, I will.'

He narrowed his eyes and nibbled his bottom lip. 'Come on. I know a way to make you feel better, but you have to keep real quiet, OK?'

'Why, what is it?'

He gripped my hand and led me deeper into the cupboard. 'Shh, you'll see.'

It turned out we were in a walk-through storage area and when we emerged out of the other doorway we were standing in the main theatre thoroughfare. The air was heavy with the scent of anaesthetic gas and the lingering, sweet aroma of the cauteriser – which always made me feel a little icky.

'What are we doing?'

Carl pressed his index finger to his lips and glanced around. He nodded to the right and tugged me with him.

It was dark and I had to be careful not to walk into any trolleys, shelves or oxygen cylinders. Carl stooped as we slunk past the doorway to the staff room. I peeked in and noticed, unsurprisingly, that it was completely empty, as was the rest of the shadowy department.

I wanted to ask him again where we were going and what the hell we were doing. It was all very covert, this sneaking around theatres in the middle of the night and, I had to admit, a little creepy.

A sudden thought struck me. Shit, he wasn't into laughing gas, was he? Because I, for one, had no intention of going on another nitrous trip, ever. The only time I'd ever indulged I'd fallen over and had needed six stitches in my scalp. I'd been a student back then and goodness knows how I'd managed to get away with that misdemeanour and carry on with my training. Beginners luck, I suppose.

'Carl,' I whispered when he stopped outside anaesthetic room three. 'I –'

He shook his head frantically, dark curls shifting messily over his ears and around his temples. He widened his eyes and pointed into the room. 'Shh,' he whispered, the hiss of sound barely audible.

A sudden, much worse thought hit me. Damn it. Was Carl the benzo thief? Was he nicking drugs from theatre as well as pharmacy? Perhaps he wasn't fussy what he took to get his highs and there was certainly plenty to choose from in anaesthetics. More than plenty. It was like being a kid in a sweet shop for a druggie, or an alcoholic hanging out in a brewery

Fuck. I couldn't believe it of sweet, funny, cute Carl. Surely not. I thought I knew him pretty well.

But what if it was? How the hell would I dob him in? A friend.

I'd have to, though. It would be that or my job, my home, my life. I would have to give him up to Iceberg and let her tear him apart piece by piece. But it would be for the best. He'd get help then; perhaps he wouldn't have to throw his career away if the problem was nipped in the bud.

I knew just about everyone at the hospital, so whoever the thief was it was bound to be someone I knew, and more than likely, friends with. But not Carl. Please no. I would never have put my money on him. Not in a million years. He had a refreshing genuineness about him, a bit flirty yes, but certainly I'd never suspected he'd been off his head on anything.

Though it wasn't exactly unknown for junior doctors to use uppers and downers to get through the first couple of sleep-deprived years after qualifying. If it was Carl he wouldn't be the first, or the last, to give into chemicals to survive.

He opened the door to the dark anaesthetic room and crept in. He tugged me behind him.

I followed, wondering what the bloody hell I was going to do if he started shooting up? What if he wanted me to?

Double fuck.

Through the watery, weak light I could just about make out a wall of eye-level locked cupboards to my left, and beneath them a cabinet that held rows of plastic containers full of all the paraphernalia the anaesthetist and his assistant would need to knock someone out. Or, as the case might be, get someone as high as a damn kite in a hurricane.

A trolley with gas cylinders, monitors and masks was pushed neatly into the corner at my right.

Carl walked right past it, with not even a glance.

Good, not the nitrous then.

At the far end of the room were two swing doors which led to operating theatre three. Each door had a small round window near the top.

Carl looked at me and pointed at the doors. He took no notice of the cupboards full of medicines. Not even a sideways glimpse. And certainly he made no move to produce an illegally gained key.

So whatever he'd brought me to do here was beyond those doors. Were there drugs kept in the actual theatre? No, everything was in here. I was pretty sure of it.

The lead weight in my stomach lifted. Carl hadn't brought me here to indulge in some illegal drug activity after all.

Thank goodness for that.

So why the hell had he sneaked us into this anaesthetic room?

He released my hand and made a zipping movement across his lips.

Completely intrigued, I nodded then followed him, almost on my tiptoes and hardly daring to breathe. Silence was clearly imperative for whatever crazy thing we were doing.

He reached the doors first, glanced through the window of the left one and turned to me with the baddest, naughtiest grin I'd ever seen. It stretched his mouth wide and balled his cheeks.

I gave him a quizzical look, and then I too peered into the vacuous, sterile theatre.

It had one downturned spotlight glowing in the corner and I scanned my gaze around the large steel objects.

Oh, my God!

I would never have believed it if I hadn't witnessed it with my own eyes.

There were two figures in the room. One in a white coat, the other in a nurse's outfit, but not a regular nurse uniform. It was way too short and had a frilly apron over the top. Like something for a fancy dress party, or even, and this is when the realisation of what I was looking at dawned on me, it was like something from a sex shop. And the pretty woman wearing it, I recognised her, had seen her a hundred times before. But never wearing anything like that, just regular pale-blue scrubs. It was Emily Smith, senior theatre nurse and all-round genius at anything to do with surgical instruments and equipment.

I drew my fingertips to my mouth to stop from exclaiming my surprise aloud, and in that moment, as the figure in the white coat turned, I saw who he was too.

Mr Ralph bloody Hartley, head of general surgery, president of the surgical council for Yorkshire, esteemed pioneer of a new cholecystectomy technique and notorious womaniser.

He wore a white coat, yes, but apart from that he was naked. A creased surgical mask sat at his throat, his slim chest was thickly carpeted with black hair, and his erect cock stuck upwards, long and thin, from a bushy mass of pubes.

I stepped backwards, stared at Carl and mouthed, 'What the hell?'

He shrugged and looked through the window again. I got the feeling he'd seen it before. How he'd stumbled upon this gem of inappropriateness between two of the hospital's most senior members of staff, including his boss, I had no idea. But I had to grant him major kudos for it, being that he was just a junior house officer and all.

Quickly I resumed my voyeurism, eager not to miss one single nugget of the extreme wickedness and what would, of course, be gold-plated gossip should I need it.

Carl into drugs. How ridiculous had I been?

'Nurse Smith, I do believe you've been neglectful of your duties,' Hartley said, strolling towards a trolley set out with various instruments. 'I asked you specifically to set up for appendicectomy not splenectomy.'

'I am so sorry, doctor. I will see to it straight away.' Emily spoke in a high-pitched, sing-song voice, not her normal tone at all. She then practically skipped towards the steel trolley, her insanely short skirt flashing white knickers as she bent and began to fuss with the silver instruments.

'It's too late for that. How will you have everything autoclaved in time for the arrival of the patient?' He stepped up behind her, his gaze going to her half-exposed rump.

'I'm sure I can, really.' She fussed with the metal implements. They rattled on the polished trolley surface, and as she fiddled she wriggled her hips, with small, inviting little movements.

'No, it's simply impossible to get everything sterilised so quickly.' He flicked up the tiny flap of material that was considered to be a skirt and exposed her twitching behind.

'Oh, doctor,' she squealed, straightening and slipping out of his reach. 'Whatever are you doing?'

He moved towards her. 'I'm going to teach you a lesson, Nurse Smith, one that you'll never forget.'

'Oh, but Doctor Hartley, I really don't think –'

'Be quiet,' he said sternly, 'and take your punishment as a good little nurse should, for I don't intend to find again that you've prepared the wrong tray for me.' He grabbed her upper arms, pulled her close, so they were chest to chest and his mouth hovered over hers. 'Are you ready to receive your punishment?'

'Oh, but –'

'Yes or no.' His voice was almost a growl; it was a way I'd heard him speak many times when he was pissed off at someone's ineptitude.

Emily melted against him, her body relaxing into his tough grip and his words having apparently taking the substance from her knees.

I would never have put the two of them together, him being at least a decade older than her and known for being a workaholic and a lothario. She'd always seemed career-focused and sensible. Just went to show, opposites attract. And this doctor-nurse game? Hadn't they had enough of the real thing all damn day?

'Yes or no?' he said again, tugging her close.

'Oh, I'm so sorry, please forgive me, sir.'

'Maybe if you take what you deserve well I'll be able to see a way to forgive you, but I won't forget. That kind of incompetence cannot be simply forgotten, you know.'

'Yes, of course, oh – Doctor –'

He spun her, quickly, roughly, and tipped her over the surgical table. With one deft flick of his wrist her knickers were half-mast and the globes of her arse bared.

'You know what bad nurses get, don't you?' Hartley said, pressing between her shoulder blades with one hand and using the other to rub her quivering buttocks.

'Yes, sir. I do, sir.'

'Say it.'

'A … a spanking, sir.'

'Louder.'

'A spanking, sir.'

'Yes, a good spanking. Ten strikes at least.'

'Ten, oh no, not ten.'

'Yes, ten. Perhaps that way you'll know not to displease me again.'

He whacked her exposed buttocks hard, with genuine male muscle behind it. The stinging sound of flesh connecting with flesh rang around the theatre as did her yelp.

'Keep still,' he ordered, flattening her when she tried to rise. 'Keep still and take it.'

'Oh, please.'

'And start counting.' He brought down another blow, to the opposite cheek this time.

Emily squealed again. Her body jerked. I felt my own bum tingle. It had been years since I'd played any spanking games.

'Two,' she said through a pant.

'No, that's one, the first was a practice.'

'Oh …' she groaned, twisting her head on the cold steel table and gripping the edge. She'd screwed her eyes up tight and rolled her lips in on themselves.

Hartley hit again, then again, his white coat flapping as he slapped and his erection jolting up against his abdomen then springing back down to a horizontal position. The look on his face was one of pure dominance; a steely set jaw, wide excited eyes and a mouth drawn into a tight, firm line.

Emily counted between yelps. 'Two. Three. Four.' She tried to stand again; her punishment clearly pained her, even in the dull light I could see colour rising on her buttocks.

'Keep still or you'll get twenty strikes,' Hartley said severely. But despite his tone he rubbed his palm soothingly over her arse, as if pacifying the blanching skin.

She moaned and widened her legs.

'Are you taking your punishment well?' he asked.

'Yes, sir, oh, yes.'

'Let me see.' He stroked down her cleft and inserted two, maybe three, fingers between her legs.

'Ah ...' she gasped, her spine stiffening.

I clenched my thigh muscles. There was no denying the fact that I was getting turned-on watching their little show. There was a heat building in my pelvis and my clit was swelling, buzzing with a rush of blood.

I glanced at Carl. He was staring through the window, wide-eyed, lips parted. I wished I could see if he had a hard on. I'd bet my last pound that he did. What guy wouldn't get stiff seeing a hot nurse spanked and fingered?

Swallowing tightly and pressing the tops of my legs together, I returned my attention to the theatre.

'Yes, you're nice and wet, taking your punishment very

well,' Hartley said, 'but you still have six more strikes to endure.'

He hit her again, a real wallop that made the flesh on her buttock ripple and shake.

'Five,' she gasped then moaned as he shunted his fingers higher, hand-fucking her pussy diligently and methodically.

More strikes rained down.

She cried out and groaned, 'Six. Seven, eight, nine.'

'Are you ready for the last one?' he asked, leaning forward and slotting his rigid cock into the cleft of her buttocks.

'Yes, oh, yes.'

'And have you learnt your lesson?'

'I have, sir, oh, I have. Please.'

'Please what?'

'Please, my last one, my last spank.'

He reared up, pulled his fingers from her and positioned the head of his cock at her entrance. He thrust into her and as he maxed out, balls deep, he struck her soundly across both buttocks.

Emily arched her back, her spine as tight as a bowstring. She opened her mouth but no sound came out. She clutched the table, trying, it seemed, to stop herself from being shunted completely off it.

I licked my lips, teeth and gums – my mouth was dry. Oh, she was getting it good. Who would have thought old Hartley had it in him to bang so enthusiastically and with such an adorable sprinkle of kink?

My nipples were tingling, my breaths coming faster. I was aware of my hips flexing ever so slightly as Hartley pumped into her, over and over. His white coat was flicking and flapping with his lurching movements. He'd gritted his teeth and was grasping Emily's hips, pulling her onto himself at the same time as he pounded into her.

'Oh, God, oh, oh …' Emily squirmed, her feet rising off the floor, her body a slave to his powerful lunges.

'Yes, yes, call me God,' he snapped.

'God, oh please, sir.'

'God.'

'God, oh, I'm coming now, please, can I, God?'

'Yes, yes come now.' He reached for her hair, a high ponytail on her crown, and tugged.

Her whole body rose. Her breasts juddered within the confines of the tiny nurse outfit, her back became a deep curve, and then she came.

The sounds of her gasping and panting through her orgasm made my knickers wet and a knot of need tightened in my stomach. Oh, she was coming good and hard. Just what I needed after the last few hours. An off-the-scale, mind-altering climax would do quite nicely to make me forget everything for a few moments.

'Ah, yes, you naughty, naughty nurse,' Hartley shouted

then flung back his head and groaned through his final strokes to satisfaction.

I shifted my feet and realised I was holding my breath and my hands were clenched into sweaty fists. Damn, I was horny for it. I wanted what they'd just had, not necessarily with the flouncy outfit and the red arse, but a damn good shagging.

I reached for Carl, curled my fingers with his, and noticed that his palm was damp, like mine.

He looked at me and gave a lopsided grin. There was a slight sheen of sweat over his top lip.

I jerked my head towards the door. It was definitely time to get the hell out, before we were either discovered or my rampant, libidinous side let loose and I hurled myself at the nearest available male.

Carl!

After a last glance into the theatre, the object of my desire nodded and we sneaked back through the anaesthetic room, out into the corridor and into the dark cupboard we'd come through.

I stopped.

So did Carl.

'Oh my God,' I whispered when the door shut, enveloping us in darkness. 'How the bloody Nora did you know they were in there, doing that?'

There was a small click and a bare bulb overhead gave

out a pale light. We were surrounded by brown cardboard boxes full of bags of intravenous fluid.

Carl released the light pull and it bounced towards the wall. He shoved his hand through his hair and puffed out his flushed cheeks. 'I had to come down here last week, in the middle of the night, to get some Gelo for Eyre Ward. I was on my own, didn't bother to turn any lights on, and went out of the wrong door, ended up in theatres.'

'It wasn't locked?'

'No, I suppose someone forgot, keeps forgetting. Anyway, you can imagine my surprise when I heard a bang and a grunt from theatre three, I went to investigate and saw old Hartley with his junk out and about to diddle his scrub nurse.'

'Jesus.' I let out a low whistle of disbelief. 'You'd think they'd go somewhere private and play, wouldn't you?'

He shrugged and ran his finger around the collar of his shirt. 'I'm guessing it gives them a kick, doing it in there.'

'You think so?'

'Yes, absolutely, catching each other's eye the next day over a patient. A theatre full of staff and only them knowing they were fucking like a couple of horny teenagers on that very table the night before.'

I shook my head. 'Yeah, I guess you're right. Must be quite a turn-on pretending there's nothing between them and waiting for the place to clear out.'

Carl looked cute as a button. His slightly unkempt, unshaven style, with his tired, bespectacled eyes and his easy smile had definite appeal.

'You'd think they'd worry, though,' I said, stepping up close and touching the askew name badge on his white coat.

'About what?'

'That someone might see them at it.'

'At it?' There was a definite sparkle in his work-weary eyes.

'Yeah, at it, screwing. They should have picked a nice, dark cupboard.' I slipped my hands over his shoulders, drew my mouth close to his. 'One with no windows, no prying eyes, or nosy colleagues.'

'Like this one?'

'Yeah, just like this one,' I whispered.

'Mmm.'

I pressed my lips to his and was pleasantly surprised by the soft willingness of his mouth and his small intake of breath.

He held my face, his big hands gentle on my cheeks and his fingers just slotting into my hair, over my ears.

The kiss deepened, our tongues tangled and I leaned my chest to his. He slanted his head and explored my mouth with a sense of passion and reverence. He tasted fresh, of water and mint. That lovely lemony scent of his that made me think of Mediterranean holidays swirled around me. A whimper of approval rumbled up from my chest and I ached for some action. I reckoned Carl was the perfect man for the job. If just his kiss had me throbbing, imagine how I'd feel when I actually got him inside me, pumping and grinding.

I slid my hands down his chest, over his pale-blue shirt to the buckle of his trousers.

'Sharon,' he murmured through our kiss.

'Carl?' I whispered, exploring lower, over his groin. I found what I was hunting for – a lovely, long hardness straining against his zipper.

'Please,' he said, releasing my cheeks.

'Please what?' I squeezed him again then gave a firm stroke, base to tip. Wonderful, he was swollen and full and I could even make out the flare of his glans through the material. How fast could we get naked?

He groaned and reached for my wrists, held them tight as I worked his erection through the material.

'Bloody hell,' he gasped, his hips rocking towards me and then away.

'You want me to suck you?' I asked, speaking against his lips.

'Fuck. No.'

I hesitated. It wasn't often a guy refused a blow job. 'You just want to shag then?'

'No, yes, I mean ...'

'What do you mean?' I kissed over his cheek, found

his ear and touched my tongue to the fleshy lobe. Cupped his balls with one hand and at the same time hunted for the zipper of his trousers and began to pull it down.

'I mean I don't, I don't want to ...' He yanked my hands upwards, so they were captured between our faces. 'I don't want to do anything.' His voice was harsh, firm.

I jolted, surprised by his sudden movement and shocked by his statement.

He was staring at me intently, his eyes wild and his lips wet from our kiss.

'Oh,' I said, shock and confusion muddling in my mind. Didn't he fancy me? Was he gay? No, I didn't think either was the case. The hardness in his pants told an entirely different story. 'But I thought ... you've got a ...'

He swallowed, the sound noisy in the small room, and then blinked, long and slow, and sucked in a deep breath.

'But you've got a –' I said.

'Tell me about it.' His mouth twisted, as though he was in pain, and he gazed intently at me.

'And you don't want to do something about it?' I licked my lips and smiled my sweetest smile. 'I'm happy to oblige. We've been putting this off for months now. You and me, naked, it's inevitable.'

'I know.'

'And?'

'And yes, I would like to do something about it, with you. Soon.'

That was more like it. I tried to step in close again but he kept me at a distance with outstretched hands. Like I was some kind of sex monster about to rape him.

'Carl?' Now he was hurting my feelings.

'I'm sorry, it's just …'

I tugged at my wrists and he released them. My body was humming. I was hot for it but it seemed I wasn't going to be getting any. 'What. It's just what?' I snapped.

'I like you,' he said, reaching out and touching my cheek. 'I mean I really like you.'

'So what's the problem?' I couldn't help my pout.

He shook his head and looked down at his feet.

'Tell me, damn it. You drag me here to watch a damn sex show that gets me all horny for it, and then bring me in a dark cupboard, kiss me –'

'You kissed me.'

'Semantics, you were into it as much as I was.' I folded my arms, tapped my foot on the floor.

He shrugged. 'OK, I'm not denying it, I've been thinking about kissing you for weeks. I can't help staring at your mouth, whenever you talk, it's just so pretty.'

He liked my pretty mouth? 'So why don't you want to take it further?' I frowned. 'What's the issue?'

'I told you.' He stepped closer.

I backed up and my shoulders hit shelving. I could go nowhere. He kept moving, until his face was near to mine, so near I could see two small freckles on the rise of his left cheek and make out the individual dots of stubble on his jawline and over his top lip.

'I like you,' he said in a low, steady voice. 'I really like you and I happen to have a rule with girls I really like.'

'What's that,' I whispered, realising that despite my irritation I was actually enjoying the fact that he'd backed me up and was looming over me with a decidedly determined glint in this eyes.

'I take girls I like out to dinner before I sleep with them.'

I nearly choked. 'You want to take me to dinner?' Damn, it had been years since I'd had a date, just as long since I'd had a normal relationship. These days it was all about immediate satisfaction. Grabbing a bit of how's-your-father when I could. It was for the best, it protected my heart but kept my body satisfied.

He frowned. 'What's so weird about that?'

'It's just …' I paused. 'Do you have a no-fucking-on-a-first-date rule too?'

He rubbed the pad of his thumb over my bottom lip. 'No, absolutely not. We can count that as dessert, if you want.'

He brushed his lips to mine and damn if I didn't get a silly little gooey feeling in my chest. Carl liked me, like-liked me, and wanted to take me on a date before we jumped into bed. It was almost romantic.

'So what do you think, Sharon? Will you allow me

to take you to dinner on Friday night? I know a really cute country pub a couple of miles from Skipton. Great food, candles, fine wine, cosy little corners and log fires.'

'It sounds like something from a soppy movie.'

'It's real life. Perhaps you just need to do something other than work and sleep so you remember what that is.'

'You can talk. How many hours have you done this month?'

'Too damn many, same as you. Which means we should definitely go and play for a while. Don't want to get dull, do we?'

My life at the hospital was anything but dull; however, the image of this little country pub Carl had conjured was very appealing. 'Friday is good,' I said with a nonchalant shrug. I didn't want him to see just how pleased I was about his invitation for a date.

'Perfect. I'm looking forward to it already.' He lifted my hand to his mouth, kissed the back of my knuckles. 'Though if my dick could talk, he'd be shouting at me for passing up the chance to get sweaty and dirty with you right here, right now.'

Chapter Four

Accident and Emergency. My heart sank. Not because I didn't like the staff, or even the work, it was just so bloody busy all the time. And there was no difference between night and day. The evil artificial lights stayed on, burning everyone's retinas, 24/7. The patients just kept on rolling in with no respect for the witching hour. And when they arrived they never slept, unless you counted the unconscious ones. They were often drunk and rarely grateful for their treatment due to the scandalous waiting time they'd endured. Who could blame them? And all that was before I remembered it was a given that none of the staff would get a break of longer than ten minutes over the entire night. There just weren't the resources.

I dumped my bag and coat in the corner of the locker room and checked my reflection in the mirror. I'd cycled as usual and my hair was a bit flat. One day I'd be able to afford a car again. One day. Quickly, I undid my hair from its band, fluffed, and re-secured my ponytail. I slicked on a little lip gloss and dropped it, and the key to my cycle lock, into my uniform pocket.

'Hey, <u>bella</u> Sharon. How are you this beautiful night?'

I would know that deep, super-sexily accented voice anywhere.

'Javier.' I turned and smiled. 'What are you doing in the madhouse?'

He gave the lopsided grin he'd perfected and scanned me up and down with a slight nod.

It was a pretty blatant once-over and despite my heart skipping, I returned the gesture.

Approval was the only verdict. The guy was an invitation to sin all wrapped up in blue scrubs and a white coat. Tall, dark and handsome didn't do him justice. It was the way he held himself, the smoothness of his skin, the coal-black sheen of his hair, the sharply slanting lines of his jaw and the ever so slightly too-big chin that gave him an air of proudness.

'I have been called to assess a surgical case. Do you know anything about it?' he asked.

'No, I've just arrived.' I walked past him and couldn't resist a nice deep sniff of his heavenly aftershave. It settled warmly in my nose and I held it there for a few indulgent seconds. 'But come this way and I'll go and find out for you.'

'Thanks, you are the best of all the nurses in this hospital.' He gave me a full-wattage smile then swept his tongue over his bottom lip.

Damn. He was hot and he made me hotter. Ever since last night, with Carl's non-starter in the cupboard, I'd been restless. Maybe I would finally get lucky with Javier tonight. If, that was, I could slink away for more than thirty seconds. He was definitely a specimen to be savoured and not rushed.

I walked into the main department, sashaying my hips a little more than I needed to and knowing full well Javier's attention would be locked onto my bum. He was a man with sex on the brain. How he'd found the space to cram all those horny neurons full of scientific facts to get through medical school was a mystery. Then again, perhaps he'd just known who to sleep with and had bed-hopped his way through his degree.

'Hello, Sharon,' Sister Taylor said, briskly wiping several names off a large white board then beginning to write new ones in. 'I hope you're feeling energetic, it's crazy down here. One out, three in.'

'Nothing unusual there then,' I said with a smile. 'Doctor Garelli is looking for his surgical referral.'

She turned and looked at Javier, gave a girly smile and touched her hair. 'Good to see you, doctor. Your patient, Tristan Bale, is in cubicle fifteen.'

'Great,' Javier said. 'Notes in the usual place?'

'Just laid open on the desk waiting for you.' She nibbled on her bottom lip and appeared to suppress an even wider smile. 'Oh, and you'll need an escort. It's a rather delicate situation.' She glanced at me. 'Can you do that, Sharon, seeing as you haven't got caught up in anything else just yet?'

'Sure.' Hang out with Javier, no problem. Perhaps I might even be able to do a little investigating about Iceberg too. See if the outlandish rumour about them hooking up was true or not.

I looked at him as he checked his pager that had just bleeped. How could it be right? She was such a wench and he was a Roman god. I just couldn't, at any stretch of my imagination, picture them together. Him taking her from behind in out-patients. No! It was like some sick joke designed to mess with my head and my stomach.

I wandered over to the desk. Picked up Mr Bale's card and glanced at his triage notes.

Oh, that was a delicate problem indeed. Rather him than me, any day. 'Bloody hell,' I said, handing the notes to Javier and pulling a face. 'What do you think he did? Sit on it?'

Javier crinkled his brow and read the card. '*Idiota* Englishman.' He stifled a yawn, covering his mouth with his hand, then sighed. 'Let's go and see what we can do about it.'

Tristan Bale lay on his side in cubicle fifteen with a thick white blanket up to his waist. He wore a fleecy red and cream checked shirt, undone by several buttons and cuffs rolled up, and his rusty-auburn hair was dishevelled on the pillow. Next to him sat a pretty woman of similar age, late twenties, wearing a sleek black leather coat and flicking through a copy of *Cosmopolitan*.

'Mr Bale?' Javier asked.

'This is him,' the woman said, glancing up from her magazine.

I hung the 'Do not disturb' sign on the cubicle entrance and pulled the curtain securely closed.

'Hello, I am Doctor Garelli, senior house officer with the surgical team on call tonight.'

'Surgical?' the woman said with a deepening frown. 'Does Trist need surgery again?'

'Again? This has happened before?' Javier asked, a tinge of surprise in his voice that matched the one in my head.

What were the chances of that?

'Oh, yes,' she said. 'Trist, you better tell the doctor about the other incident. So he knows what a bloody fruitcake he's dealing with.'

I looked at Tristan, who swallowed tightly. His long face was pale and his fingers were knotted together so tight the tendons on the backs of his hands stood out. He wore a wedding ring and his fingers were marked and calloused, by the looks of them they were hands used to hard labour and cold weather.

Javier flicked over the chart, and I peered along with him to see what Mr Bale's vitals had been on admission.

Normal.

Even so I was concerned about the pastiness of his skin so I reached for the blood pressure machine and quickly checked he was still stable. He was. That was good; it meant his pallor was less likely to be down to haemorrhage and probably down to bossy-wife syndrome.

'Mr Bale, would you like to tell me how this has happened?' Javier asked.

Mr Bale glanced at his wife. His lips tightened and he gave a small shake of his head.

'Maybe,' I said, giving Javier a meaningful look, 'it would be best to examine Mr Bale first.'

'Yes, good idea, that way I can go and get a coffee,' his wife said, stabbing the *Cosmo* into a red Prada handbag and standing. 'I have no intention of hanging around this husband of mine while you all look at his rear end and wonder what you're going to do with him.' She tutted and then, with a flick of the curtain and a swish of leather, she was gone, her high heels clicking into the distance and melting into the noise of the department.

Carefully, I secured the privacy of the cubicle again.

Mr Bale gave an audible sigh.

'Are you OK?' I asked, resting my hand over his. He was a nice-looking guy, a sprinkle of freckles over his long, straight nose and a strong chin that held a hint of pale stubble.

'Not really, but a bit better now I don't have to listen to her caustic remarks.' He shook his head. 'That's all I get these days. Is it any bloody wonder I go to the lengths I do to get a bit of pleasure?'

'Well, you do realise this search for pleasure has landed you in a rather precarious situation, don't you?' I said gently.

He shrugged miserably and averted his pale-blue eyes from mine. 'I know, but I couldn't help myself.'

'Do you mind if I examine you now?' Javier asked, snapping on a pair of gloves.

'Go ahead, doctor, feel free.'

'I'll take this blanket off then,' I said.

Beneath the blanket he was naked. His knees were together and bent, his backend sticking out.

'I'm just going to take a little look,' Javier said. 'OK?'

'OK.'

Javier tugged Mr Bale's uppermost buttock.

'Good, there is no bleeding so that is an excellent sign,' Javier said, tipping his head.

Mr Bale groaned and shifted.

'No, keep still,' I said, resting my hand on his knee.

'Keep very still,' Javier repeated and applied some lube to the tip of his middle finger. 'I am just going to have a feel. Do not bear down. The last thing we want is for you to clench.'

'Easy for you to say,' Mr Bale said, squeezing his eyes

105

shut and wearing a look of absolute concentration. His lips turned snow-white he was pressing them together so hard.

Javier furrowed his brow in concentration and looked at me. 'It's pretty high up but I think it's intact.'

'Good,' I said calmly.

'It's a screw-in,' Javier said.

'Oh.' Did that make a difference? I didn't think so. 'That's good then.' I gave a small non-committal shrug.

Javier gave me a look. One that Mr Bale couldn't see but said what a total crackpot we've got here.

I gave another small shrug. He was, but our patient obviously had his reasons. And who were we to judge?

'Right,' Javier said, withdrawing and snapping off his gloves. 'I'm afraid there is only one option and that is surgery. There is no way we can risk it coming out naturally. Chances are it would reach the sphincter and shatter. That would mean a colostomy, which I am sure you are keen to avoid.'

'Yes, absolutely.' Mr Bale nodded frantically. 'I definitely don't want one of them bag things.'

No, of course he didn't. How would he get his jollies then?

I covered him back up with the blanket. 'Doctor Garelli will take very good care of you, Mr Bale.'

'Please, call me Tristan. Everyone does.'

'OK, Tristan,' Javier said. 'Now I need to go and

organise a theatre and the consent form, so I will leave you in Nurse Roane's capable hands.' Javier flicked off the tap and grabbed a paper towel. After tossing the towel in the bin he walked up close to my side.

Again his scent enveloped me. I couldn't help but be impressed by how tall and broad he was and the sexy way his dark hair licked the collar of his white coat.

'And while Tristan is in your very capable hands,' he said quietly, 'will you get a psych history for me?'

'Sure,' I said, resting my fingers on his arm. It wasn't my job to get a patient history but I would do the basics for Javier. 'Shouldn't be a problem at all.'

'Great,' he said. 'I owe you one.'

'Mmm, I guess you do.'

He narrowed his eyes and appeared to suppress a grin. 'I'm not a man who likes to be in debt.'

'Good, because I don't like waiting for what I'm owed.'

He chuckled then exited the cubicle.

A warmth spread in my belly. Yes, I was getting pretty close to doing the deed with the hospital hunk. If I could just clear up the matter of him and Iceberg first, get him to confirm that it was all a sick rumour, then it would make the occasion so much more fun.

I turned to Tristan. He was nibbling at his thumbnail, his eyes wide.

I reached for his notes. 'Please, don't look so worried. By morning we'll have you all sorted. You'll probably

107

even be able to go home, as long as there is someone to keep an eye on you.'

'I think Nadia, my wife, will go and stay with her sister for a while after this. She said something about that on the way here.'

'Does she live nearby, the sister?'

'Hull, not too far.'

I jotted this down in his notes. It was too far. He'd have to stay in longer if he was going home alone. 'And do you work?'

'Yep for myself. I'm a farmer.'

'And Nadia is your next of kin?'

'Yes, I guess so.'

'Any kids?'

'No chance.'

I raised my eyebrows, surprised at the vehement tone in his voice.

He sighed. 'That's how all of this started.'

'All of this ...?'

'Shoving things up my bum. Yeah, that's why it started. Nadia decided she didn't want to have sex any more after she accused me, wrongly, of carrying on with another woman nearly a year ago. Damn long time for a man to go without any ... you-know-what.'

'Yes, absolutely.' Blimey, nearly a year. That's got to be hard on anyone, but for a nice-looking young farmer in the prime of his life? Not fun and quite likely to push him into an affair if he wasn't having one before.

'Thing is,' he said. 'When the bloody hell would I have time for another woman? I work all the daylight hours God gives me, seven days a week. Hardly conducive to shagging around. But she wouldn't let up, kept on and on about the girl at the tractor shop until she'd created this wild, passionate romance in her head. It was just a figment of her imagination. No grounding or truth to it at all.'

'But you must have told her that. Reassured her?'

'Yes, course I did. Over and over. But she wouldn't believe me. In the end I think it must have sent me mad or something.' He sighed. 'I keep telling her that I work all day, every day, for her. To buy her nice things, keep a roof over our heads and make a home for the kids we hope to have one day. But will she listen, no. Fat chance.'

'So how did this, er, problem start?'

He was quiet for a moment, then, 'Don't think I'm not embarrassed about this, because I am. And telling you, a young woman, about my stupidity, is humiliating. Not something I'd planned, ever.'

'Don't be embarrassed on my behalf, Tristan. I've seen everything over the years working here.' This was a first. But I wouldn't tell him that.

'I'm sure you have.'

'So tell me,' I said, drawing up the chair his wife had used. 'Right from the beginning. I really need you to be specific, for the notes.'

He sighed. 'OK then. After all this affair fuss Nadia took to going to the new gym in Skipton. Suited me fine. Then one day, about two years ago, I'd popped back to the house to make a sandwich for lunch and the doorbell went, it was one of those City Link vans, the collies were going nuts. Anyway, the guy handed me the box so I signed his little screen thing, and he went away. I wasn't expecting anything, so I was intrigued.'

'What was it?'

'It was a prize, some competition I didn't even know I'd entered. Maybe I hadn't and it was just a random thing. Whatever it was it was free and it changed my life.'

I raised my eyebrows. 'Oh?'

'Sounds crazy,' he lowered his voice, 'but it was a box of sex toys. There were blindfolds, handcuffs, pink feathery ticklers and a spanking paddle. Vibrators too, with lube that tasted of strawberry.'

I suppressed a giggle. 'So what did you do with it?'

'Well, I just shoved it in the tool shed to start with. But then after a few days I went back to it. Had a fiddle, you know, with the vibrator and the, er ...' He frowned. Tristan?'

'The butt plugs. There were two – I didn't know what they were to start with, had to read the leaflets that came with them. Well, eventually curiosity got the better of me, it wasn't like I was having sex. Nadia's legs were firmly shut and she was sleeping in the spare room

110

until I confessed to sins I hadn't even committed. So you can imagine I needed some kind of release, or stimulation at least. Most of the stuff there was for couples to play with – except the plugs. Well, I could do that on my own. So the next time she went to her step class, I got the lube and the butt plug and carefully eased it in.

'The thing was big and that was the smallest of the two. It hurt but not in a bad way, in a good way. Kind of stretched and burned and then when it eventually popped in it felt amazing. I loved it instantly, that feeling, and my dick got hard.' He touched his cheek; there were small dots of redness beneath his freckles. 'I'm sorry, I shouldn't be telling you things like this.'

'It's fine. In fact, more than fine. You need to tell me so that we can help you.'

He swallowed and glanced away.

'Please, go on. How did it escalate?' I asked.

'It escalated fairly quickly. I was like a guy on Viagra when I had a plug in, it really hit the spot. Not that I got to share any of that new-found libido with anyone. This was all done on my own. Soon I couldn't wait for Nadia to go to the gym so I could grab that plug and play.

'Then one day, I discovered something. Nadia was supposed to be going to see her sister, the one in Hull. I pleaded paperwork jobs; I wanted an hour playing with my toys, undisturbed, before I had to plough the twelve acre field. Nadia had got just far enough away for me

111

to get a plug in and then she came home. I was upstairs when I heard the door. I felt sick. Quickly, I pulled up my jeans, shoved the lube in my sock drawer and then walked down the stairs. The plug shifted inside me with each step – it felt amazing, hard and solid on whatever it is up there that's so sensitive. But more than how it felt inside me, was "knowing" that it was there. My secret. That was thrilling. She'd accused me of being secretive, well, now I was. Kind of served her right.

'So I opened the mail while she ranted about the car's new rattle and how she didn't trust it to make the journey to Hull. I said I would take a look and all the time I was hard as concrete, the plug doing its job regardless of Nadia's constant disappointment in me. I felt hot and feverish with excitement. If only she knew that her husband had a big butt plug up his arse and a raging hard on that would rival any porn star's.'

'But she found out, eventually,' I said.

'Yes, and it was my own fault, really. I got greedy.'

'How come?'

'Within a few weeks of that day I was wearing a plug nearly all the time, not just in the house but out on the farm. That constant state of arousal became the norm. I liked it – it made me feel alive. No, more than that, it made me feel when I hadn't felt anything in months. Eventually though I decided I wanted some more, bigger, better plugs. I'd heard you could get vibrating ones. I fancied that, could just imagine how great they would feel. I wondered if they were silent and I'd be able to sit watching *EastEnders* with Nadia in the evening, buzzing away and her know nothing about it.

'So I dug out the details of the place that sent me the original toys and went online and put the order in. I spent nearly two hundred pounds. Bought whatever I fancied. The bigger the better, ridged were great and so was anything that had a battery.' He frowned. 'Now don't get me wrong, nurse, I'm not gay. I didn't buy anything that vaguely resembled a penis, that isn't what this is about. If another bloke tried to shove his cock up my arse I'd deck him. I think of women when I'm aroused, sexy, hot, naked women.'

I nodded seriously. I could see that was a big deal for him. He might be a fruitcake but he was a straight fruitcake and that was important.

'I had a wonderful time with all my new toys. I liked one called the Bionic Bullet the best. It was a good size but when it started vibrating it was awesome. Had me stiffer than a bull's horn I can tell you. But each plug had its own merits, its own advantages. My favourite, though, was a thick squat one – it was made of glass and seemed to stay cool, even when it had been inside for a while. It was perfect for wearing for a long period of time, through dinner with the family, or watching one of Nadia's soppy movies in the evening. It kept me hovering

113

in a nice state of arousal for hours until I could go and relieve myself in the bathroom before bed.'

'So what went wrong?' I asked. 'How come you've done this to yourself today?'

He shook his head, shifted slightly. 'Nadia found my stash. It was a Wednesday, I got back from the weekly market expecting ham and eggs, and instead my plugs were all set out on the kitchen table.'

Nice. 'Did she know what they were?' I asked.

'Yes, she's not stupid. She hit the roof, went into the fridge, grabbed the ham I was supposed to have for my tea and threw it to the dogs. She then stormed off and I didn't see her for several hours.

'I put the plugs away and hoped that was the end of it. She would either come back for her designer wardrobe or not. That suited me as well as anything, I guess I'd pretty much given up on her.

'But she did come home. Silent and moody, and as soon as I went out to check the cattle she got rid of all my back-entry treasures. Every last one. I was upset. But what could I do? If I bought more I knew she'd find them, dispose of them again, or maybe worse, serve them up in a casserole pot for Sunday dinner when we had the family round. I wouldn't put anything past her, the mood she's been in.

'So that's when I began to experiment. That full feeling, the arousal, the secret in my arse had become a habit – no, more than a habit. A need. When my bum was

114

empty, I was empty. Sounds strange to say it but I kind of felt bereft.

'Then, not long after, I was in the bath and my attention fell on a bar of soap. Next thing I knew I was easing it in. Felt bloody amazing after a few weeks of being empty. I got out of the bath feeling like myself again.

'Best thing was Nadia had no idea and I didn't need to worry about hiding anything. I replaced the soap with a fresh bar on the side of the bath and that was it, I was ready to go downstairs to watch *Silent Witness*.

'Except what I thought was good really wasn't. My guts began to growl and spasm. Then it was all I could do to get up to the bathroom in time to expel the soap. Didn't feel nice, I can tell you. But despite my discomfort I knew I was on to something. I just needed to find home-made objects to slip up there. Nothing chemical, that just hurt, and nothing that wouldn't be able to find its way out if I couldn't grab it.

'I fashioned a couple of plugs out of candles, they were pretty good. Vegetables were fine too, but didn't last that long, and let me tell you, ginger root burns to high heaven. If anyone ever offers you a ginger root butt plug, think twice. How hot do you really want to be?'

'I'll bear that in mind,' I said, making a mental note and also hoping I'd never be in the situation where I'd have to use the information. 'So how did you end up needing a doctor the first time?'

He sighed. 'I'm a bit of an obsessive type of person. Always have been, so thinking up new ways to plug myself became my every waking thought. Nadia knew none of it, or if she did she turned a blind eye. Until, that was, I made the mistake of using one of her Impulse perfume bottles. I think it was Hint of Musk, quite a nice one. It went in fine and had a good length, felt pretty substantial as I moved around, sorting out some feed deliveries. But then later on, I realised it was stuck. But not only was it stuck, the damn thing was leaking. I was farting perfume, smelt like a bloody pansy. This all happened right as Nadia came out of the bedroom hunting for her Impulse. I couldn't hide my distress, I was farting yes, but the damn sprayer must have been going off all the time. My guts were filling up with gas of an unnatural kind.'

'That must have been awful,' I said, making a concerted effort to keep my face straight. This poor guy really was an act-now-think-later kind of bloke.

'Well, she took one look at me, put two and two together, guessed my secret and called the ambulance. I felt that was a bit extreme, after all, I only had a perfume bottle stuck up my arse, wasn't like I was in a car crash or anything. But I wasn't really in any fit state to argue. I didn't know whether to hop about, lie down, or try and poo it out.'

'Sounds terrible.'

He shook his head. 'It was. And never again. It was the first time I felt scared of what I'd done to myself. And then when they had to sedate me, pull it out … I was pretty embarrassed.'

'But you're back here now? Why?'

'Yeah, I'm a tosspot, aren't I?'

'Well, I can see you have your own reasons for doing this, but still.'

'I was self-controlled for ages after the Impulse affair. But then it started up again. Just a shampoo bottle when I was in the bath at first and then a carrot when *Strictly Come Dancing* was on. Nothing seemed to quite hit the spot though, do you know what I mean?'

'Yes.' No. 'So what happened today, for you to take such a risk again?'

He sighed, closed his eyes for a long moment then opened them again. They held a look of defeat and resignation. 'Earlier me and Nadia had another row about that woman in the tractor shop. Apparently the new John Deere 5GH series is in and she called and left a message to let me know. Well it was a make or break row, neither of us can continue the way we are, living in virtual silence and as strangers. Let's just say the conversation didn't go well and afterwards I went into the tool shed, sat down and my attention fell on a box of spare light bulbs. The top one looked just like one of my old plugs. Smooth, a good size and a tapering shape. The next thing I knew I was circling the pointy end around my bum-hole. I told myself out loud how stupid it was, but then, because of the lube I suppose, it was in. Damn thing felt good, a solid wedge of pressure right where I needed it. I got hard instantly, breathed through the lovely sensation and stared out of the shed window at the sunset.

'It wasn't until I stood that a wave of panic washed over me. Damn thing felt so delicate inside me and it was sliding higher. I'd been a prat yet again. And this time I knew it could be the end of my arsehole forever if I didn't get some serious help.'

'You were right to come straight here.'

'Well, Nadia guessed what I'd done as soon as I very gingerly walked into the kitchen. She didn't say a word, just got her coat and handbag and ordered me to lie down in the back seat of the Land Rover, on my stomach.' He shrugged and shook his head. 'And now you poor people have to deal with me.'

'Everyone makes mistakes.' I rested my hand over his. 'But once this is over, once the surgical team extract the bulb, then what? Will you stop?'

'Yes, I won't ever do it again. Not now.'

'I do really think this should be the last time,' I said, 'with home-made plugs, at least. It sounds like they're the ones that land you in the most trouble, physically.'

He sighed. 'Yeah, but Nadia won't allow me to have proper ones.'

118

'Then you need to get inventive with your hiding places, or else just buy one plug and keep it hidden ... you know where, all of the time.'

'Mmm, maybe you're right.'

'But mostly, you need to have a long talk with Nadia about her lack of ability to trust. How about going for some marriage counselling? Do you think that would help?'

'I don't know if anything will. She hates me.'

'If she hated you she wouldn't still be at home cooking and watching TV in the evening with you, and she certainly wouldn't have been concerned enough to drive you all the way here on a wintery night. I think another, impartial person moderating a proper, honest conversation might get things back on track for you both, in and out of the bedroom.'

His face brightened a fraction. 'You can get people to do that?'

'Yes, of course, that is what marriage counselling is. Would you like me to get you the information on where to go for that help?'

'If you could, that would be great. She might finally see sense. If she'll come with me that is.' He shook his head and his face fell again. 'Which I doubt.'

'I get a feeling, from what you've told me, that she does still love you, and if that's the case then I'm sure she'll want help. But there is obviously something else

going on in her head, something that needs examining.'
I paused. 'Maybe she's been cheated on in the past.'

He creased his forehead into a deep frown. 'She has, her ex was a total ratbag to her for years. She couldn't believe a thing he said. Prick.'

'There you go. There are trust issues she needs to face and then come to the understanding that not all blokes are cheats.' But lots are ratbags, I added silently as my heart subjected me to a familiar pang of loss. 'And learning to trust again is a slow process, no matter who you're with. It's like having a glass vase shatter and trying to carefully piece all of those shards back together again, in just the right place as they were before.'

'But I've never cheated on her and never would. Hell, I couldn't believe my luck when she married me two years ago. A beautiful woman like her, wanting to spend her life on the farm with me. I thought I'd died and gone to Heaven.'

'And I'm sure she couldn't believe her luck.' I rested my hand over his. 'Stick with it, get some help and you never know, the rest of that box of toys you won, it might just come in useful after all.'

He managed a half smile and I looked up as Javier opened the curtain. 'Is theatre all set?' I asked

'Yes.' He flashed a winning smile and strolled in. 'Good news, I have spoken to Mr Hartley, the consultant on call, and we are going to use sedation to remove the foreign object. That will make for a much quicker recovery period and you'll be able to go home by sunrise.'

'Oh, that's good,' Tristan said.

'As long as all goes well.' Javier frowned. 'Which we can't guarantee and is why the procedure will be carried out in the operating theatre, just in case there is a ... er ... mishap with the glass and more extensive surgery is required.'

'Yes, absolutely, whatever you think, doctor.'

'Did you get some history?' Javier asked, turning to me.

'Yes, a little.'

'Great.' He held the curtain open and made a small gesture with his hand for me to exit the cubicle.

I smiled at Tristan. 'Theatre staff will be here in a few minutes to collect you and I'll get that information put in your notes, you know, the name and numbers of who to call to get some mediation.'

'That would be great, and, you know, thanks for listening.'

'You're welcome.'

Once outside the cubicle, Javier cupped my elbow and steered me to one side. 'What did you learn from him?'

'That he just can't help himself. It's a compulsion.'

'Do you think he needs a psychiatric referral?'

'Marriage counselling more like. He needs to find a different way to cope with his distrusting his wife rather than shoving things up his bum-hole.' A sudden image of

Javier and Iceberg flooded my mind – them together in out-patients, her bent double and him ramming in from behind. His stethoscope swinging, white coat flapping and his buttocks clenching.

I looked at Javier now and I just didn't believe it. The guy was super-hot and far too suave for a bitchy cow like her. Would he really?

'You ever done it?' Javier asked, a wicked glint in his dark, velvety eyes.

'What?' I knew damn well what he was talking about, but a naughty part of myself wanted to hear him say it.

'You know, up the arse?'

I pretended to look indignant, though it was hard when his looming proximity was doing funny things to my knees and his aftershave was once again messing with my thought process. 'No,' I said. 'I have a perfectly good part of my anatomy that does the job just fine.'

'Sensible girl,' he said, reaching out and tucking a stray strand of hair behind my ear. He let his hand hover on my shoulder, his fingertips just brushing my neck.

'Why? Is it your thing?' I asked as a tingle went over my scalp.

He shrugged. 'To have something in my rectum, no.'

'How about to dish it out?'

'No, I'm like you. The traditional way is perfect.' He lowered his head. 'And did I ever tell you I think you are perfect?'

I laughed. 'Now you're talking rubbish. If you knew me at all you'd know that I'm far from perfect.'

He looked hurt. Oscar nomination hurt. 'Sharon, nearly two years we have worked in this hospital together. I know you very well, and I do indeed think you are perfect.' He slipped his finger from my collar to the indent of my throat. 'Your pretty eyes, your luscious blonde hair, your lips so kissable. And how you smell, your slim ankles in sexy stockings, the curve of your neck, the list goes on and on.' He made some kind of appreciative click with his tongue. 'It is all so perfect for me. You are perfect for me.'

'That's very sweet of you to say so.' He was a grade-one flirt that was for certain. But it was OK, because I'd given myself a personal mission to shag him asap and it seemed he had the same thing on his mind.

'I am a sweet guy.' He grinned teasingly. 'So perhaps if you are looking for a foreign object to insert you will think of me.'

Shocking! I twitched my eyebrows. 'Maybe I will. Italy is part of the EU but still foreign to a Yorkshire lass.'

He leaned a little closer. 'Let's get to it soon. You have made me wait so long I ache, right here in the depth of my heart.'

'In your groin more like.'

'Nurse Roane. Doctor Garelli.'

A sudden, all too familiar, sharp voice, shook me from

my moment of being flamboyantly, if slightly ridiculously, wooed. I turned and saw Iceberg standing with her hands on hips and a flush on her cheeks, staring at us from the middle of the department. 'Have you nothing else to do but hang around all night chatting?' she asked.

'Lisa,' Javier said, stepping away and holding out his hand towards her. 'I was just thinking of you.'

I suppressed a laugh. Damn the guy had no shame. If he didn't have the Armani looks to go with his smooth tongue he'd be heading to the stocks for a shower of rotten tomatoes and soiled incontinence pads. The nurses here just wouldn't put up with it. Me included. You didn't need to be a genius to know that everything that came out of his sexy mouth was sugar-coated crap.

'Mmm, it didn't look like you were just thinking of me,' Iceberg said, glaring my way but her voice softening as Javier approached.

I folded my piece of paper into my pocket and tucked away my pen. I didn't catch her eye. She had enough against me as it was; giving her extra ammunition wasn't sensible, even in my book.

'I most certainly was,' Javier said. 'I am taking a patient to theatre and I needed to let you know that if things don't go to plan we will need a surgical high dependency bed.'

'Mmm.' She looked suspiciously at him. 'Really.'

'Yes, you know that you are always the one I go

124

to when there is something I need.' He gave another award-winning smile then glanced at his pager which was ringing. 'Damn, I have to nip to Eyre Ward before I scrub up.'

'OK, I'll catch you later,' she said with a smile.

'Yes, later.' He turned.

'And let me know about that high dependency bed,' Iceberg called after him, her voice all light and breezy as she gave a little wave.

Yes. She had it bad for him. But was it reciprocated, or was he just using her affection to keep his life easy? Get the senior night nurse on board and he'd have a sweet ride through his time here. It was a sensible plan.

'I will,' he said as he strode across the department. His shoes clacked on the floor and his loosely opened coat swished. He caught the attention of staff and patients alike as he went, all probably wondering what snazzy US medical drama he'd floated in from and where the camera crew was hiding.

'Well?' Iceberg said, folding her arms and her voice as hard as stone again.

I glanced at a man with blood dripping from his nose. He was trying to take a sip of tea; it wasn't going well. 'What do you mean?'

'Well, do you have anything for me?'

'I don't know what you're talking about.'

'Sharon,' she said, hissing my name like a snake being

trodden on. 'Don't play dumb with me. Do you have any information yet, anything at all on who might be messing around with the benzos?'

'No.'

'Well, while you're flirting with senior house officers who are completely out of your league, you would do well to remember that Personnel won't wait forever, and when they get twitchy I'll put your head on the block to save my own. Let them wade through the paperwork your gross misconduct will produce to take the heat off my problem.'

Out of my league – bitch. I clenched my fists and made myself think carefully before I spoke. No point telling her that the flea-ridden rats at the local dump were out of her league. That wouldn't keep my job safe. I took a deep breath. 'I'm sorry. I've had my ear to the ground, really I have. But it's so busy, there's no time to pick up any gossip or figure out anything that's going on. Besides, here they have their own more than adequate stash of temazepam. If it was a member of A&E staff, theirs wouldn't be tallying.'

She frowned. 'Mmm, well it's a good job you're heading up to Bennett Ward then. They've had someone go off sick. Bloody Nicola, pregnant again and throwing up all over the place. Why that girl can't say no to her husband or get herself on the pill is beyond me.'

'What? You want me to go up there now? With all

this going on?' I gestured to the man with the bloody nose who was now trying to help another patient with a revoltingly swollen right foot and something that looked suspiciously like a dinner fork protruding from his toe.

'Yes, now. And be sharpish about it. They're busy too.'

Chapter Five

After settling three patients on Bennett Ward, young guys who'd had a particularly rough time, I headed to the nurses' station. Rachael was still busy with the drug round and the two healthcare assistants were chattering in the office.

I picked up the desk phone and dialled Carl's pager number. It only took a couple of minutes for him to call back.

'You paged Doctor Rogers,' he said, bewilderment in his voice that Orthopaedics was contacting him at midnight.

'Carl, it's me.'

'Sharon?'

'Yes.'

'You OK?' He stifled a yawn.

'Did I wake you?'

'Fat chance, I'm just out of surgery. Some nutter shoved a light bulb up his arse. Took me and Javier forever to fish it out.'

'Did you?'

'Yes, I managed to get hold of the slippery sucker just when Javier was losing patience and said we'd have to open him and perform a colostomy. I had one last go, didn't dare squeeze too tight with the forceps, but at the same time it was so bloody high up his rectum and it just seemed to be wriggling deeper. I had no choice but to get a decent grip and hope for the best.'

'And you got it?'

'Yes.'

'Great.' I thought of Tristan and hoped he'd buy himself a proper butt plug and make a phone call to the marriage guidance office in town.

'So why did you call?' Carl asked.

'I need to speak to you, about tomorrow night.'

'You're not ditching me, are you?' There was humour in his voice but also apprehension.

'No, not at all. I'm looking forward to it.'

'So why do I sense there's a "but" coming?'

'There isn't.' I paused. 'Well there is, kind of.'

'And?'

I wasn't quite sure how to say it, he might flip, spectacularly. But, after the conversation I'd just had it was a risk I had to take.

After taking a deep breath I blurted the words out. 'Do you mind if we take a group of patients into town instead?'

'What? Are you serious?'

'Yes, but it's not what you think. They're nice lads and have had a really horrible time since their car nose-dived into ditch a couple of months ago.' I hesitated, knowing Carl would think I'd lost the plot.

He said nothing and his silence confirmed my suspicions. He'd likely put the phone down in about five seconds time. I couldn't help myself, though. My heartstrings had been tugged almost to snapping point by the boys' pleas.

'I've looked after them on several occasions,' I went on, my words tumbling out, eager to explain before he gave up on me altogether. 'They're much better now, not ready for home or anything, but they've been given a pass for one night to celebrate Tim's birthday. They just want a non-hospital meal and a couple of pints, nothing wild, not when they're all in wheelchairs.'

There was a pause then, 'Can't their family or friends take them?' He sounded more disbelieving than shocked and I hoped that was a good sign.

'No, they're from Essex, no visitors tomorrow. Besides, the pass is on the condition they're accompanied by nurses.'

'Well, surely orthopaedic nurses can do it.'

'Apparently one is, but they need two.' I sighed and shook my head. 'They've just given me a long, convoluted story about how they've been asking everyone all day and I'm their last resort. If I don't do it, it's a no go.'

Carl sighed. 'So it has to be you?'

'And you too, we need an extra wheelchair pusher, plus we can still have a meal out together, a glass of wine and all of that. It will be fun, same thing, just more of us.'

'But I've booked at table at The Thatcher, eight o'clock.'

Damn, I could hear the disappointment in his voice, but it didn't match the despair in Nick, Tim and Johnny's earlier, plus it was three against one. 'Can we change the booking to next week?' I asked.

'I suppose.' He sighed again. 'If we're not working.'

'I'm off on the Saturday, even better.'

'You really want to do this?'

I hesitated, because it was more than a want, it was a compulsion, a real calling to do the right thing. 'Yes,' I said quietly. 'They deserve a treat and I can make it happen. Besides I think they'll be hurling themselves out of the window otherwise.'

I could picture Carl sliding his finger and thumb beneath his glasses and rubbing the bridge of his nose, the way he often did when faced with a problem.

'In that case,' he said, 'and if it's what you want to do, who am I to argue?'

A sweep of relief washed through me. 'Thanks, Carl, you won't regret it, and it's still a date.'

'No, no, it's not a date, not by any stretch of the

imagination, but …' He paused. 'I will still enjoy your company, even if I have to share you.'

'Here we go,' Carl said, setting down a tray holding four brimming pints and two glasses of Chardonnay.

'Cheers, doc,' Nick said, reaching for a beer. 'This is the best medicine by far.'

'Oh, I've been dreaming about this,' Johnny said, holding a pint by his lips and inhaling the scent of the beer.

Rachael, the nurse from Bennett Ward, passed Tim his pint then reached for her wine.

'Cheers,' I said, holding my drink to the centre of the table. 'Happy birthday, Tim.'

'Happy birthday,' everyone chorused.

'Thanks,' Tim said. 'And here's to a whole evening of hospital freedom. Bliss.' He clinked his glass against Rachael's and took a deep drink.

Carl looked at me, grinned then supped on his own pint.

I relaxed, finally. The trip from the hospital to town had been stressful using a minibus taxi, and then finding our way through a rapidly filling pub to a table we could slot three wheelchairs around hadn't been easy.

It was a pub-slash-club. The music was loud, the lights dim. On the way through the guys were head-level with people's bums and groins – not that it seemed to bother them. Most of the girls were dolled up to the nines. Skirts

132

so short they were practically belts, and with the onset of the cooler months extra layers of fake tan had been applied, though in the shadows the streaky ankles and wrists weren't too noticeable so they looked reasonably golden.

'What's this place called?' Nick asked.

'Heaven and Hell,' I said.

'Great name, and definitely Heaven for us tonight, it's crackin'.'

'So you like it?' Carl asked.

'Yeah, it's cool. The music is OK, the beer cold and the talent isn't bad at all.' He flashed an approving smile at a girl wearing a skin-tight fluorescent blue dress. She grinned back, tossed her hair extensions over her shoulders and pulled a lip gloss from her purse.

'Sharon tells me you're all from Essex,' Carl said. 'Does that make this your first experience of Yorkshire lasses?' He looked between them.

'Yeah, never really been out of Essex, me.' Nick's attention was still on the bright beauty.

'So how come you were on the A614 when you had the accident?' Carl asked.

'We all had a few weeks off and were just bumming around. So we came up with a vague plan to head to Newcastle, see what the nightlife was like there; then drive up to Edinburgh, you know, catch some comedy shows at the Festival maybe. Just as well we hadn't booked loads of hostels or things to do, because it all came to a sudden halt when that knob landed his balloon on us.'

'Did they offer to transfer you to a hospital in Essex?' Carl asked.

'Yeah, it was mentioned, but I had to go back to theatre twice for my pelvis and it made sense to stick with the same surgeon. Tim and Johnny could have gone but they opted to stay with me. Great blokes.'

'The best,' I said.

'And then Tim got an infection and no other hospital was going to welcome him with open arms.' He shrugged. 'So that's just how it's been, our wonderful trip to Yorkshire to see the inside of a hospital for two months.' He reached out his hand to Carl. 'I know you put your date with Sharon on hold to come out with us tonight, so thanks, mate, we appreciate it.'

Carl took his hand and shook it. 'No worries, just make the most of it, because I'm not cancelling that table for a second time.' He looked at me and grinned. 'Not for anything or anyone.'

I got a lovely warm feeling in my belly. Not just a I-wanna-rip-your-clothes-off feeling, but something more – like satisfaction without having been satisfied. It was a delicious sweetness to know that I was wanted for more than just bed action, but for my company and my conversation too. It wasn't that I couldn't have had a more meaningful relationship in the last few years with someone, I could have, but no one had caught my interest enough to want more. Michael had been the only one for so long and I couldn't imagine replacing him.

But Carl ...

He was getting to me. Something about him had penetrated my armour, made me think of a future with someone again. Perhaps it was because here he was on one of his precious nights off, helping me with this crazy plan. He had a good heart, and a gentle soul.

The music switched to a song I recognised from the charts. My feet twitched, my shoulders bobbed. 'You want to dance?' I shouted to Carl.

He shoved his glasses up the bridge of his nose and nodded. 'Yes, OK.'

'Stay here,' I said to Nick in my sternest voice. 'Do not go anywhere, any of you.'

'I'll keep an eye on these bad boys,' Rachael said with a giggle then nudged Tim.

'I haven't even begun to get bad,' Tim said with a decidedly wicked glint in his eyes.

Rachael giggled a bit more and reached for her wine. I wasn't sure, but through the shadows I was sure a blush had risen on her cheeks.

'Come on,' Carl said, 'I like this one.' He led me through the throng of people towards the small, crowded dance floor, holding my hand tight and tugging me behind him.

135

Once there, he turned and began to dance with enthusiasm. I joined in, trying my best to control my rhythm amongst all the shoulders and hips bumping into me. There was barely room to move, the air was hot, the music vibrated from the floor to my feet, through my chest and into my head. But I wasn't complaining. It was so good to be out, having fun.

Carl was a cool mover. I wasn't surprised that a few admiring glances slid his way from the girls dancing around us. He definitely had that certain something and his squarish glasses and unshaven chin just added to the appeal.

Soon I was hot, my thin pink top warm against my skin and my hairline tingling with perspiration. I was just about to suggest we go and sit down when the music switched. A much slower beat that rumbled through the air and into my body. Like magnets, the dancers around us came together in pairs.

'Don't think you're escaping, little lady,' Carl said, sliding his hands around my waist and pulling me close. 'You're the one that wanted to dance.'

'And I still do,' I said, slipping my hands over his shoulders and linking my fingers at his nape. Beneath his dark-blue shirt he was solid and a memory of us in the cupboard, kissing hungrily, came to my mind. I suppressed a tremor of longing and pulled in the fresh scent of his aftershave. Yep, I still wanted him as much as I had then, if not more. 'Have you been here before?' I asked.

'No, I've not really been out since I arrived. Either working or too knackered.'

'So how do you know about The Thatcher?'

'My parents came up last month. We went for Sunday lunch there. It was really nice and I thought then you might like it.'

'You thought that a month ago?'

He shrugged, appeared a little bashful. 'Well, yeah, it took a bit of courage to ask you out.'

Damn, he was making me melt. 'That's so sweet.'

'No, not sweet. I just wasn't sure if you were single or not. I had to ask around.'

'Oh, did you?' Shit. I hoped to hell he hadn't uncovered any of my wayward night-time antics. But I doubted it. I might enjoy a good, no-strings shag, but I was pretty careful and I knew full well my mortuary mate, Tom, wouldn't have said anything. Not with a ten thousand pound wedding about to happen.

'I didn't want to step on anyone's toes, and a girl like you ...' He stroked the back of his thumb down my cheek. 'Funny, pretty, dedicated, intelligent, I was certain someone would have snapped you up for themselves.'

My cheek tingled where he'd touched me. 'No, no snapping.' Just a bit of naughty fun. 'So what about you? Why no lady in your life?'

He put his hand around my waist again and I became aware of my breasts pressing into his chest. I liked the stretched, leanness of his body, there was something very masculine about it despite the fact he wasn't distended with muscles.

'There were some girls, at uni.'

'Which medical school did you go to?'

'Oxford.'

I gave a low whistle. 'Impressive.'

'It was what was expected of me.'

'Who by?'

'My parents. They're both Oxford-bred consultants. As their only child, they expect me to achieve the same.'

'That's a pretty high star to hitch your wagon to.'

'So far so good.' He nibbled on his bottom lip and my attention was drawn to the soft plumpness of his mouth and the way the disco lights flashed across his stubbled chin. Damn kissable.

'I bet they're really proud.'

'I hope so.'

'So tell me about the girl, at Oxford.'

'Girls, in the plural. I had several long-term relationships during my five years studying. All sweet, a few a bit too intense. None that I wanted to continue seeing on qualifying. So it's been good to get away. I feel like I've finally grown up. The student thing was getting old at twenty-eight.'

I raised my eyebrows. Twenty-eight?

He shrugged. 'I had a rather extended gap year, touring Australia with a couple of mates. It was too much fun to come home.'

'Sounds great.'

'It was. But eventually I had to get my head into the right place for medical school.'

'Do you have any idea what specialty you want to end up in?'

'Dad's a urologist and Mum's a gynaecologist. So I'm thinking surgery. This first rotation has been fun even if Javier spends most of his time checking out nurses' backsides, but Mr Hartley, despite his spanking tendencies, has been really patient and a good teacher as I've got to grips with wielding a scalpel.'

'Good, I'm glad.' I paused. 'That was shocking the other night. When Hartley and Emily were going for it in theatre. Who would have thought?'

He ran his hand up my back, slipped his fingers into my hair and lowered his head. 'Yeah, they were behaving incredibly badly.'

'Did it turn you on?' I asked.

Our lips were so close, just a whisper away. His breath warmed my mouth and cheeks.

'You know damn well it did. If I remember rightly you felt the evidence of that.'

I did remember, only too well. Carl had been having

some serious space issues in his trousers. Shame he'd been so stubborn about letting me help him out with the problem.

I sighed and touched my lips to his, leaned into him. We fitted so well together, our mouths, or bodies.

Instantly he took control of the kiss. I shut my eyes. Became lost in the slightly malty flavour he was gently feeding me with his tongue. The lights penetrated my closed lids, the music boomed in my ears, but all my senses were focused on Carl. My skin tingled for his touch, my mouth craved more, and as he breathed out I breathed him in.

Yes, it had definitely been a very long time since I'd wanted anyone as much as I wanted Carl. I had a feeling that he'd be quite a dark horse when unleashed. If only he would just allow the stable door to be opened.

Eventually he broke the kiss. 'We should go and check our charges,' he said, pushing his glasses back into place. 'Make sure they're behaving.'

The music had changed, to another fast-beating track, but I hadn't noticed until now. I'd been so wrapped up in Carl. Every stroke and lick of his tongue had made me forget where I was. 'Er, yes, you're right, we should.'

He smiled and I wondered if he realised just how much he'd gotten to me. More than any other bloke for ages. And it wasn't just his body I was after, it was his kisses, caresses and smiles too. Being with him felt right.

Not that things hadn't been right in my life before I met him, I'd been fine being single. Since Michael I hadn't wanted anything serious, but now, I definitely felt better than OK when I was with Carl. I felt great.

We wound our way back towards the table, my thoughts spinning about this new, deeper level of attraction I was feeling for the man holding my hand. I watched the way his shoulders shifted beneath his shirt as he moved, how three creases pulled taut between his scapula, and how his hair tumbled over his collar, a few curls sticking up since I'd just run my fingers through them. A little thrill that he was mine, that those little licks of soft, ruffled hair were mine, for this evening at least, warmed my chest.

Arriving back at the table, I saw the guys had been ordering food. Several plates of chicken and chips were set about as was a whole stack of crisps, dips, garlic bread and creamy mushrooms.

It smelt good and I reached for a hot, fat chip, blew it and munched.

I stopped mid-chew, my mouth inelegantly open. What the?

Tim was leaning half out of his wheelchair, holding Rachael by the shoulders as he kissed her thoroughly. She seemed quite happy with the arrangement and was reciprocating with equal enthusiasm, her palms placed on his chest.

141

'Whoohoo, Tim's getting lucky on his birthday,' Nick shouted then wrapped his arm around the girl in the florescent blue dress he'd been giving the eye to earlier. She was sitting on my chair sipping from a vodka-mix drink bottle. She looked in no hurry to go anywhere. I'd lost my perch.

Next to her was another girl, in Carl's seat, wearing a similarly ridiculous dress and holding Johnny's hand.

'Everything still works down there,' Johnny was saying to her. 'I'm only in a wheelchair because of my ankle, nothing wrong with my todger.' He pointed at his groin and grinned. 'It can get up and go with the best of them. Full working order.'

Bloody hell. Five minutes was all it'd taken for them to hook up. And Rachael and Tim? I should have seen that coming.

I reached for my purse, took a slug of Chardonnay and spoke into Carl's ear. 'I'm just going to the ladies', back in a minute.'

I squeezed and apologised my way through the crowd. Eventually I came to the restroom, which had a picture of a female devil on the door, and escaped the thud of music.

After visiting a cubicle, I re-applied a slick of gloss, ran my fingers through my hair and squirted on my favourite perfume, Cashmere Musk. Oh, bloody hell. I would have to use this bottle up and then find a new fragrance. Musk reminded me of Tristan with the bottle of Impulse up his bum. He'd totally ruined it for me. The thought of him farting out that musky spray was enough to put anyone off it for life.

'Sharon.'

I turned. It was Rachael. Her cheeks were flushed and her eyes wide.

'I feel terrible,' she said. 'That shouldn't have happened. Oh, what am I going to do?' Tears brimmed on her lower lids.

'What do you mean?' I asked, dropping my perfume back into my purse.

'Tim. Me and Tim. I know you saw. You're very kind to pretend you didn't, but –'

'Hey, it's none of my business.' I held up my hands and shook my head.

'But it's misconduct, against the rules.' She clasped her palms over her cheeks. Two fat tears dripped down her face, dragging with them a smear of mascara. 'How could I have risked my job? I worked so damn hard for that qualification. You could go right ahead and report me to Iceberg or Personnel. In fact, you should, right now. It's what needs to be done.'

'Hey, hey, you're getting your knickers in a twist,' I said, plucking a tissue from my bag and handing it to her. 'I'm not going to say a word to anyone, least of all Iceberg or Personnel.'

'I don't want to get you into trouble for withholding information though,' she said, sniffing loudly.

'One thing I've learnt over the years, Rachael, is knowing when to keep my trap shut, and this is definitely one of those times. I couldn't give a stuff about withholding information.'

'But if anyone finds out there'll be an investigation, a tribunal, the R will have to get involved, so will the Nursing and Midwifery Council. It will be a nightmare. I'm so ashamed of myself.' She sighed theatrically.

'Really?'

'Yes.' She frowned. 'Don't you realise how serious it is to have a sexual relationship with a patient? It's totally forbidden. Frowned upon by everyone.'

'Have you had sex with Tim?'

She looked horrified. 'No, of course not.'

'Then why are you worrying?'

'Don't you see? The intent is there. We're attracted to each other. We "want" to have sex.'

Intent, for crying out loud! If she could see some of the intents I'd had over the years that had turned into thoroughly scandalous, real life, actions. There was no doubt in my mind Rachael would keel over in shock. Blimey, imagine if I told her about my most recent shag on the autopsy table, and damn, she'd probably have a straight out heart attack if she knew I'd given a patient a handjob a few nights ago, just to make him feel better.

'I really think you're making a big thing of it,' I said, leaning towards the mirror to check for stray mascara.

She blew her nose. 'Do you?'

'Yeah, a kiss, for heaven's sake. No one here will say anything, so as long as you play it safe until Tim's discharged then you'll be free to hook up.'

Her shoulders sagged and she let out a deep sigh. 'Do you think so?'

'Sure, worse things happen than two people being attracted to one another. Don't sweat it.'

She reached for her lipstick and began to fix her well and truly smudged outline.

We were silent for a minute then she said with a smile, 'He really is a seriously talented kisser.'

I grinned. 'He's a great guy. You'll be good together.'

A dreamy glaze went over her eyes. 'He says when I walk onto the ward it reminds him why he fought to stay alive when they were in that awful ditch. He didn't know my name or what I looked like, but the minute he saw me it all fell into place why his life had been spared.'

'I didn't realise he was such an old romantic,' I said with a grin. I liked Tim. He wore his heart on his sleeve and I could see why Rachael found that so appealing. Not to mention his blond, surfer-dude looks and buff body. He was a bit on the thin side at the moment, but he would soon bulk up again once he was able to move about.

'So was it instant attraction?' I asked.

'Yes, he might have been lying in bed all smashed up but I still thought he was gorgeous.'

'Ah, that's sweet.'

'Well, not everyone would think lusting after a patient was sweet, but you just can't help it when someone captures your heart in a way no one else has before.'

'No, you can't. Not at all.' I thought of how I was tumbling into a new dimension when it came to my feelings for Carl. 'I guess you'll just have to go with it and hope for the best.' Which was exactly what I was telling myself to do. Looking back at the past wouldn't do me any favours, I had to look to the future and be positive, optimistic. 'So was that your first kiss?' I asked. 'Out there in Heaven and Hell?'

'Yes.' She touched her lips, as though remembering his against hers. 'And it just kind of happened. He pulled me close when I reached to put my wine down. I see him in bed so much I forget that he's a pretty big guy, and strong too. Damn, I want to go and do it again, but I shouldn't, I know I shouldn't.'

'In for a penny in for a pound,' I said. 'If anyone finds out, which they won't, you're not going to get into any more trouble for two kisses than one.' I rested my hand on her shoulder. 'If I was you, I would go back out there and kiss your man's socks off.'

She grinned. 'Yes, you're right, and he could be discharged as early as next week. All being well.'

'Go easy on him when he does get out, though,' I said.

'What do you mean?'

'In the sack, don't go bouncing on top of him and fracturing him again, will you? All this pent-up sexual frustration, waiting for each other for months, things could easily get wild.'

'Sharon.' Her eye's widened. She appeared genuinely shocked.

I shrugged. 'I'm just saying. He's going to be a bit delicate for a while, not to mention out of practise. You'll want to start off slow, perhaps with a blow job just to get it out of his system without putting too much pressure on his spine.'

'Really, I –'

'Come on,' I laughed, 'we'd best get back out there. They'll be wondering where we've got to.'

'Yes, we should.' She gave me an odd look, then had one last glance in the mirror, rolled her lips in on themselves and checked her teeth. 'So you and Carl. Is it serious?'

'No,' I laughed. 'This is the first time we've been out. But we hit it off as friends months ago, when he arrived.'

'He seems really nice, though I don't know him well. He doesn't have any need to visit Orthopaedic.'

'He is nice, really nice, and he's genuine, not like some doctors.'

'You mean like Javier Garelli? Blimey, his reputation

precedes him. I should think they're bracing themselves at St George's for his arrival.'

I looked at her quizzically.

'I did an extended surgical placement last year. I grew to love and hate him.'

'Yes, I know what you mean.' Well, you couldn't help but love his body, his cheesy lines ... well, yes, I could see how they'd get old if you worked with him all the time.

'He was pretty cranky too and thinks he can get away with it because he's God's gift.'

'Cranky? Really?'

'Yeah, if he wasn't flirting he was complaining about not being able to sleep and snapping everyone's heads off. We never knew what mood he was going to be in when he stepped onto the ward. We took to bracing ourselves and tiptoeing around him.'

That surprised me. The Javier I knew was a gold medal player, but he was also pretty chilled.

'Perhaps he's sorted out his body clock, finally,' she said, pushing open the door to the din of the club. 'Which will be good, it'll make everyone's life easier.'

We arrived back at the table to find Nick and Johnny locking lips with their two new female friends, and Carl and Tim deep in conversation about the latest football results.

'Hey, I missed you,' Carl said with a grin and holding out my wine. 'Come cosy up with me.'

I was happy to. And as the next hour or so passed in a rush of banter and laughter within our group, the sensation of having Carl's leg pressed against mine and his arm on the back of my chair was nice, safe almost. I exhaled for the first time in months. I would worry about those missing benzos and Iceberg's threats tomorrow.

Until then, I was off duty.

Chapter Six

The rest of the evening went well. The Essex boys had a great time and like three gruff Cinderellas they were heading back to the ward before their wheelchairs turned to pumpkins. As we rattled across the car park Rachel and Tim disappeared and had a quiet smooch behind a van. I made a point of saying to Johnny and Nick that what happens on a hospital night out, stays on a hospital night out, and it really was best to keep their lips zipped about Tim and Rachael's romance.

They got my drift, and besides, they were too excited about their own conquests, who were, apparently, coming in all their fake-boob-fake-tan glory to visit them on the ward the next afternoon. I hated day shifts the way most people hated toe fungus, but I would have suffered one to see Staff Sister Ermintrude's face when they appeared to visit her most unruly long-stay patients.

Carl and I dropped Rachael at her place and then finally, at half past midnight, he drove me home.

'Aren't you coming in?' I asked, when he failed to kill the engine.

He leaned over, tilted my chin with his index finger and breezed his lips over mine. 'I don't think that would be a good idea.'

'I think it would be a great idea.' I was really fancying a bit of naked Carl to sort out the ache I had for him. Damn, it was becoming uncomfortable. Want and need an itchy, spine-wriggling sensation that was building each time we touched. 'Come on, we've been on a lovely date, let's go have coffee.'

'By coffee you mean a shag?'

'Well, if you insist.'

He laughed. 'You're great, perfect. I love a girl who knows what she wants.'

'I want you.' I ran my fingers into his thick hair, drew his face to mine again.

'Mmm,' he said, 'so damn tempting.'

'So don't resist. What's the point?'

'I told you. I want to take you for dinner first. Forgive me for having a sense of tradition and for being an old-fashioned kind of bloke, but tonight wasn't a date. I told you that.'

'We had dinner.'

'A couple of chicken drumsticks and chips. That was sustenance, not real food.'

'So I'll make you an omelette.'

'Nice try.' He took my hands from his hair and set them in my lap. 'Dinner at The Thatcher, next Saturday, and afterwards ...'

'Afterwards?'

'Then afterwards maybe we can take this thing further.'

Bloody hell, a whole week before any rumpy-pumpy action, I would implode with frustration. For goodness sake, he was a doctor, wasn't he supposed to make me feel better, not worse? 'Well, we'll see,' I said, roughly clicking off my seatbelt and opening the door.

'Sharon.' There was surprise in his tone.

'Playing hard to get doesn't suit you, Carl.' I reached for my purse and stepped out.

'Hey, I'm not. I just want it to be special. I told you, I really like you.'

'We've known each other for months, have flirted, watched an impromptu sex show, been out tonight, dancing, eating, drinking, kissing. How damn special do you want it to be?' I slammed the door.

Instantly the electric window whizzed down. 'Don't be like that, you know what I mean.'

'Maybe I do, maybe I don't.' I turned and headed towards my flat with my lips pressed together tight. I was mad as hell. I knew I was, and I didn't trust myself to speak when I'd gotten so angry that little black spots invaded my peripheral vision. Carl had made me feel a fool for wanting him. Treated my turned-on state like it was something to be toyed with, mocked almost. That was something I just couldn't handle. I might like sex more than most but that didn't mean I'd given up on pride.

Sure he'd said he wanted me too, but what kind of man turned it down twice? Twice?

There was a perfectly good bed in my flat, no one to disturb us. No urgency to get back to work. I was burning for him and unless my arousal antennae were seriously off, he was hot for me too.

Perhaps he was gay after all. Private school, Eton no doubt, had probably given him a taste for it and he just needed a girl as camouflage as he climbed the career ladder. Couldn't have a penchant for bumming holding him back, or depriving Mummy and Daddy of the son they wanted to brag about at dinner parties.

Well, I wouldn't be camouflage for anyone. I wanted a full-frontal relationship or nothing at all, and Carl was running out of chances pretty quickly. Yes, I was more attracted to him than anyone else since Michael, but that didn't mean he could walk all over me. No way. Not going to happen.

As the entrance to my block slammed shut, I heard his sporty little car drive off.

Sod him.

It was his loss.

Ophthalmology was the dullest ward in the hospital. In fact, it only needed to be open overnight occasionally. Usually, as had happened today, because a list had run over and patients who'd had general anaesthetics needed to stay in for observation.

But apart from a few eye-drops and the odd cup of tea there wasn't much to do. I was working with Matilda, the most ancient of all the night nurses and one who could do the ophthalmologist's job better than he could himself, she'd been in the specialty for so many decades.

Great thing about Matilda was she was quiet. She didn't chat. She was happy to bury her head in a Mills and Boon, knit hats for the baby unit or, if she was feeling like a challenge, puzzle at Sudoku.

Which left me to wallow in my misery, or was it frustration? I wasn't sure, but whatever the hell it was, I'd been spun into an emotion that didn't sit well and was making me feel quite nauseous.

'So how is everything here?'

Oh, great, the icing on the cake. My favourite senior nurse.

'All settled and stable,' Matilda said, not even bothering to put down *The Billionaire's Virgin Bride* when Iceberg walked up to the desk.

'Good, just what I like to hear.' Iceberg settled her eyes on me. 'So you won't mind if I take Staff Nurse Roane for a while. I have something I want her to do.'

'Fine.' Matilda lifted her book back to her nose.

As if life could get any worse. The last thing I needed was Iceberg digging in her nails tonight. I didn't think I could take it. I already felt like I was in an emotional tailspin without her blasting off about my misconduct.

'So, staff nurse,' she hissed as we walked from the ward.

'What?'

'Any news.'

'No, I wasn't even on duty last night, and now here, with the least likely person in the whole entire hospital to ever even consider nicking benzos. Seriously, it's like you don't want me to find anything out.'

'Of course I do, and if you want to keep your job you'll be even more anxious to discover who the culprit is.'

'And how do you suggest I do that, stuck in ophthalmology with Matilda?'

'You're not stuck in there any more. For the next couple of hours I want you to have a snoop around. Lurk near pharmacy, see what you can see. It's been two weeks since anything went missing and I'm pretty sure whoever it is will strike again soon.' She held up her mammoth bunch of keys. 'See this little silver one.'

'Yeah,'

'Someone has a replica of it. I need to know who, sharpish.'

'But what if they never go back for more? I could be hanging around for years watching the cupboard.'

'They will. One thing I know about druggies is they're greedy. One hit is never enough. One stash and they always need more. It was a Saturday night last time it was taken. I reckon between midnight and three. Go and skulk around.'

I resisted rolling my eyes. Though the minute she turned, I did just that. Seriously, go and hang out in dark corners and shadowy doorways for three hours, just in case someone had a replica key? Was this really all I was qualified for?

Turning, I heard Iceberg walking away, no doubt off to terrorise some other poor soul.

Bugger it. My mood was as black as the night outside. Just when I thought it couldn't get any worse it did when a sign for Rose Cottage generated a tug of sadness in my chest. Tom would be married by now. Today was the big day for the big boy. I should be happy for him and I was when my mood wasn't so dark, because it wasn't that I wanted him for myself. I just liked his incredible dick. Not only was it a perfect specimen, he was a master at using it. I hoped his new bride was coping with him tonight. From what he'd said over the year or so we'd been banging, she wasn't particularly accommodating of his size, tended to do a lot of squeaking and squealing and crossing her legs.

She'd just have to learn, and when she did, boy would

she be glad she'd put the effort in. She'd have a smile on her face for the rest of her life.

The theatre department still had the main lights on. I guessed all the lists were running over, either that or something had come through Accident and Emergency. Carl was working. I knew he was because Hartley's team were on call, so he was no doubt in there, scrubbed up, doing his stuff.

I didn't give the theatre a second glance. He could apologise to me. He'd have to if he still wanted to keep the table booking at The Thatcher. Otherwise, well, otherwise, he'd blown his chances instead of getting blown himself.

Dumb guy with his old-fashioned values. Seriously? The walls we worked within might be Victorian but we weren't.

A rattle and the rhythmic clatter of fast footsteps caught my attention. I turned and saw Sister Taylor rushing towards me with a porter. They had a female patient on a trolley, who was groaning and moaning and clutching her enormous abdomen. An anxious, about-to-be father was jogging at her side, gripping her hand and swiping at his brow.

I pressed into the wall to allow them to pass. Sister Taylor gave me the briefest of smiles – she was clearly anxious about getting to the maternity unit before the delivery. The porter, the new young guy who'd helped me to the mortuary with Mr Parslow, looked about to break into an Olympic sprint. I got the impression that although he didn't enjoy moving dead bodies around the hospital it was preferable to women in the final stages of labour. He should maybe re-think his career.

They turned the corner and I was left alone on the long corridor. Silence wrapped around me once again. The nights were quiet, especially after one o'clock, but still, anything could happen.

Mooching along, I finally came to the pharmacy. Cupped my hands around my eyes and peered through the dark window on the dispense hatch. I only ever saw pharmacy shadowed like this and without the frenetic activity of the day – the bustling laboratory geeks measuring out micrograms and milligrams, fussing over contraindications and side effects.

I liked it quiet. Rows upon rows of medication all neatly labelled and ordered. Everything you could possibly need and very little in there I wasn't familiar with, except perhaps some of the chemo drugs and the fertility drugs – they were for day clinics. I never went there.

Satisfied all was as it should be, I headed towards the maze of back corridors. Directly behind the pharmacy there was a small room, kind of like an office, but with a sofa bed. If the on-call pharmacist was brought in for some reason they used it. But as far as I could tell those occasions were few and far between. I'd made good use of it just after

Michael had left and I had hooked up with a hunky porter called Raif. He'd been charming and gentle, knowing that I was just out of a long-term relationship. Trouble was, eventually he'd wanted more and I'd just wanted his hot body. Too many years with the same person had made me curious to find out if I'd been drawing a short straw.

Turned out I had. Raif was incredibly skilled with his tongue and I managed to convince myself that was a positive for Michael and I splitting. If we hadn't, I wouldn't have spent dozens of happy night-time breaks receiving oral sex in that pharmacy room. Unlike Michael, Raif never seemed to get tired of doing it. His tongue had the stamina of a racehorse; it could run marathons and twist like some spinning ride at the fair. And one orgasm was never all I got. The first fast hard one was just the starter for several more slow-building, gloriously deep climaxes that made me want to scrunch up into a ball at the same time as flail my arms and legs wide.

A little tremble attacked my belly at the memory. It was a damn shame he'd wanted more from me. We'd connected in the sack, but apart from that we had nothing in common. I'd never had a long conversation with him. It was just a series of texts arranging to meet. My pussy had stared at his face for more hours than I had.

I opened the door to the room. It was warm, dark and peaceful. Perhaps I could use it to hide out for a couple of hours.

Flicking on the small desk lamp, I looked at the sofa. The thought of flopping down, perhaps flicking through one of the *Country Life* magazines on the desk, then having a doze, was very appealing. I yawned and stretched my arms out to the sides. Yes, a lie down would suit me well. After last night's late arrival home and then a fitful sleep that had resulted in an early morning masturbation session, I was pretty exhausted today.

I sat, dropped back onto the sofa, and as I did so all my worries came knocking on my brain. What the hell was I going to do if Iceberg carried out her threat and went to Personnel? I'd lose my job; in fact, I'd lose my registration, of that I had no doubt. Chances of finding one of those bigwigs in London who shared my compassion for a helpless, aroused man were slim to none.

Then, without my regular wage, I'd run behind on my loan repayments and the mortgage. I'd have the flat repossessed, have to sell everything and declare myself bankrupt. My only choice would be to head to Mum and Dad's, which wasn't really an option since they were in Spain living out their retirement in a one-bedroomed apartment. No, I'd be on the street. No one would care. Not a soul. Michael was long gone. I had friends but not one firm friend who I could crash with.

The shit was about to hit the fan big time, and I couldn't see any way of avoiding it.

I bit back the desire to cry. What good would that do?

Nothing. There was only one thing for it and that was to get Iceberg off my back once and for all. I would have to be her damn bitch and do her snooping. Find out who the hell thought it was OK to dip into the drug cupboard whenever he or she wanted to.

I stood, snapped my uniform straight and squared my shoulders. I was made of better stuff than this. I would not be defeated by an impromptu handjob, an evil witch and a druggy-thief. I'd worked too bloody hard to get to where I was and to be self-reliant and independent.

Silently, I slipped from the small room. My gaze fell on the corridor light switches. Perhaps if I dimmed them that would make any light-fingered individual feel more secure, and in turn, I'd be able to seize my moment and catch them in the act. I fingered my iPhone in my pocket. I'd take a photo of them with their hand in the cookie jar and then show it to Iceberg, that should do it.

After reducing the corridor lighting by half I wandered up to the large, grey metal cupboard that was the solution to my dilemma. 'I wish you could tell me who else opens you,' I whispered, stroking its cool surface. 'It would help me out no end, you know. Maybe if you can speak, only once, you could do it now.'

The cupboard was bolted to the wall, its doors securely closed. It remained stubbornly silent.

'Hey, *bella* Sharon.'

'Javier.' I spun around. 'You scared the crap out of me.'

'I am sorry.' He pressed his hand to his chest. 'I wouldn't make you feel bad for anything in the world. My only desire is to make you feel good.' He waggled his eyebrows. 'More than good.'

'What are you doing here?' I asked, thoroughly appreciating the way he filled out his pale-blue scrubs – a scribble of chest hair poked from the V in the top, his impressive package bulged and his white coat was left wide open.

'I have come to have quiet five minutes in that little room over there.' He pointed to the pharmacy office. 'I discovered it a few months ago. Perfect for sneaky little interludes.'

He stepped closer and his aftershave clung to me like some weird kind of hypnotising drug. 'Yes, it's a very useful little room,' I managed. 'Have you just come from surgery?'

'Yes, a complex hemi-colectomy. Kept bleeding every time we tried to close.'

'Not fun.'

'No, not at all, but perhaps ...' He placed his finger on the back of my hand and traced a delicate line up to the crook of my elbow. 'You would like to join me in my interlude?'

Really?

Now?

Damn that tug in my belly was back, that furiously insistent pull that was demanding satisfaction with flesh and not some silicone moulding.

Javier's offer was tempting. More than tempting. It seemed like a great opportunity after my recent let-downs by Carl.

But I was supposed to be watching the cupboard.

'Sharon, why do you look so worried?' he said, sliding his hand up my arm to my shoulder. 'You do not think I will show you a good time?'

'It's not that,' I said. 'I just …' OK, so maybe I could leave the cupboard for half an hour; but I had to ask him about Iceberg. What was going on between them? I didn't want her secondhand goods, that was enough to put me off the whole idea.

'Just what?' He leaned closer, slid his other hand around my waist.

'Javier.' I pressed my palms against his hard chest, his pectoral muscles solid rises of warm flesh beneath my hands. 'I just need to know, there's this rumour, you see.'

'A rumour?'

'Yes, about you.'

He pulled back, looked down at me, his lips a straight, tight line. 'So tell me. I do not like the fact that people talk about me.'

'Well …' Why did the words feel like they were stock-piling on my tongue? Buck up. Just say it.

'Sharon?'

'You and Iceberg,' I blurted. 'I mean, Lisa Stanton, you know, senior night nurse.'

163

'What about her?'

'Are you shagging her?'

'What?' He stepped away as though I'd just electrocuted him. Raised his eyebrows and shoved his hand through his luscious thick hair. 'My goodness, no, people are really saying that?'

'Yes, lots of people. Apparently a porter saw you at it, in out-patients.'

'Well, that is ridiculous.' He stepped away, rubbed his hand up and down his face. 'Completely untrue. Why would the man say such a thing?'

I could have punched the air with relief. Of course it was untrue. The whole idea of him and Iceberg was preposterous.

'And people believe this lie?' he asked. 'That there is a romance between me and her? I don't mean to sound unkind, but she is not really my type.'

My thoughts exactly. 'She isn't?'

'No.' He stepped closer again, cupped my cheeks in his palms. 'For the record, you are my type. Sharon, I have wanted you for so long. Too long. It pains my heart that we are both too busy to spend time together.'

'So why am I your type?'

'I have told you before. Pretty and intelligent, and your body, I just want to worship you, hold you in my arms and feel you melt against me.'

I looked up into his dark eyes. He had beautiful long

lashes and skin like silken caramel. Melting against him seemed like a reasonable option for the next half an hour.

'OK,' I said, touching his smooth cheek. 'Let's take that interlude.'

The right side of his mouth twitched and a flash went across his eyes. 'Ah, my *bella*, you won't regret.' He linked his fingers with mine and led me the dozen steps back to the pharmacy office.

I'd left it in darkness, and Javier didn't bother to turn the light on when we went inside. Instead, as soon as the door shut, he swept me into his arms and kissed me with fervour. I pressed my body into his and the evidence of his arousal shoved into my abdomen.

Finally, some action. Good, solid action by the feel of it.

I pushed his white coat from his shoulders, heard it land on the floor. He tugged up the skirt of my uniform and roamed his hands over my satin knickers, tracing the outline of my buttocks without once breaking the kiss, his tongue an insistent force searching my mouth.

Damn, he tasted delicious; spicy and rich, maybe with a hint of coffee. Not like Carl's fresh, sweetness.

Carl!

'Ah, baby, you are a doll in my arms. I want to love you so much,' Javier whispered into my ear, his accent thicker than usual. 'So perfect, so delicious, you are my every fantasy come true.'

165

'Really?' I was a little breathless his kisses were so enthusiastic.

'Oh, really.' He groaned. 'I am so hard for you. So long being so hard for you.'

That hardness was straining at my hip but I had other ideas of where I wanted it. I tugged at his top, pulled it over his head and threw it on the floor. 'Condom,' I gasped.

'Yes, here. In my wallet.' He released me, stooped, scrabbled, then was up and over me again.

I shoved at my knickers, felt blindly for the sofa and dropped down onto my back. Damn, I was hot for him. Carl had teased me once too often. All this rubbish about dates and dinner and being old-fashioned.

Carl!

An image of him hovered before me in the darkness. I could hear Javier breathing heavily as he rolled on the condom. He didn't sound like Carl, not his voice but not his breathing either. And he didn't smell like Carl.

I wondered if Carl would take off his glasses to make love. I'd never seen him without them. Not that I was complaining, they were sexy in a way that was newly appealing to me.

'*Bella*, where are you? It is so dark,' Javier said, shuffling towards me. He touched my arm. 'Ah, there you are. Come here, let's finally be as one.' He moved over me, his heat, his smell, his weight, all folding down on my body, suppressing me.

I suddenly felt as though I'd been punched in the chest. My breath stuttered and a rise of panic made the hairs on my nape spike.

Shit. I don't want to do this!

Those words flooded my mind. It was like having someone shout them loud and clear. But the shout was in my voice and held a note of anger.

A realisation of what I did want flashed in front of me. Bright and gaudy like Las Vegas sign-lights, the clarity of the message could not be ignored.

I wanted Carl. Just Carl.

Having Javier inside me would be no better than the vibrator. A substitute – Quorn not beef, water not wine.

I wanted more than this. I wanted to believe in the person attached to the sex drive. For so long I'd been using guys for their appendages and between-the-sheets talent, but not any more. That had to stop.

Carl had gotten under my skin. He'd wormed his way into my head and, dare I admit it, my heart too.

The thought of Javier kissing me, entering me, just didn't appeal the way it used to. I liked Carl kissing me, Carl holding me, dancing with me, talking to me.

Damn it, he'd ruined everyone else for me.

The sudden change in my mindset was too powerful to ignore. I had to get out of there. Ditch Javier and go and apologise to Carl, see if I could salvage what we'd started together.

My first instinct was to clamp my legs shut. But when I tried I realised that Javier was already settled between my thighs.

'No,' I said, trying to sit.

'Yes,' he murmured, connecting his chest to mine and finding my mouth. 'Ah, yes, so sweet.'

I shoved at his shoulders. Tore my lips from his. 'Javier. I've made a mistake. I can't do this.' Bloody hell, why was he so big and heavy? It was like having a damn concrete slab lying over me.

'Yes, you can do this. Yes, I am big but not so big that you won't be able to take it.' He stroked my hair. 'Don't be scared of Javier's penis, just relax and let it in.'

'No, no, it's not that.' As if!

'Let me give you great pleasure, *bella* Sharon.'

'But I don't want to, I'm … I'm with someone else.'

'Well, he is not keeping you satisfied if you are here with me.' He prodded my entrance with the tip of his cock. 'Let me do his job for him. I will make you more satisfied than you have been ever before.'

'No, I can't, please.' I shoved harder, tried to twist away. Months of anticipating, dreaming of this moment and now it was the absolute last thing I wanted. I felt sick, panicked. Jesus, was this rape if I'd wanted it until the final moment before penetration? I didn't know, but what I did know was that I had to get him off me.

168

I kicked, twisted my body, put all my strength into pushing his shoulders.

'Sharon, *bella*, what are you –?'

A sudden wild beeping filled the small room. Fast and furious, an insistent, manic alarm. It was his pager. The rapid, loud tone indicating that he was needed urgently, patient-about-to-die urgently.

We both stilled.

Surely he wouldn't ignore it.

'*Cazzo!*' Javier said, his dense weight lifting. '*Cazzo*, my *bella*. The timing could not be worse. I have to go.'

Relief washed over me. Never before had I been so glad to hear that crazy noise. Usually it instilled dread. Someone was critical. It was a call to action. But not right now. Now I was hugely grateful that it had come to my aid. Javier had been big and powerful over me, sheathed up and about to plunge.

Maybe he would have stopped when my pleas registered.

Maybe he wouldn't.

I'd never know. But it had been a close call and my breathing was rapid and my pulse rattling in my chest. I drew my legs together, wrapped my arms around my waist and remained seated on the sofa, hugging myself tight.

Javier was hopping about and cursing in the absolute darkness. I heard the rustle of material, his brisk breaths and a few more Italian curse words, then the door flew open.

169

A dribble of light trickled in as his footsteps beat into the distance.

I saw my knickers abandoned by the bin and reached for them. As I tugged them on I spotted Javier's wallet on the floor next to a purple condom wrapper.

Grabbing both, I stood. He'd probably gone to attend to the patient he and Carl had been operating on. The person who'd kept bleeding in theatre. Poor bugger.

I should get Javier's wallet to him though, as soon as possible; then I could avoid him until he went to St George's. There was no way I wanted a repeat performance of what had nearly been a completely disastrous half hour in an otherwise totally rubbish night.

Disastrous?

Yes, disastrous, dreadful, catastrophic.

I had to admit it. My once-shattered heart was on the mend. Not only that, it was beginning to beat for someone new. Someone sweet and charming, clever and with a future we could maybe share.

Standing in the doorway, I heard more thudding footsteps. They were coming from the opposite direction to the way Javier had taken off.

I paused, wondering which one of the crash team it would be. I'd stand still so that I wouldn't get in their way.

A figure with wild hair, a flapping white coat and black glasses careered around the corner. He looked like a train about to go off the rails, his feet going faster than his body, his arms windmilling. With an outstretched hand he steadied himself on the wall and then hurtled towards me, head down.

Carl!

Shit.

He spotted me, skidded to a halt, his shoes making a squeaky, braking sound on the polished floor.

'You seen, Javier?' he panted.

'Yes, he's just gone that way.' I pointed. 'About ten seconds ago.'

'Great. I didn't fancy being the only surgeon to respond.'

'No, he's just ahead of you.'

'Good.' He looked about to take off again but hesitated, his attention on my hand. The one I was using to point the way.

His mouth opened. No words came out.

Double shit!

He was staring at Javier's wallet, but not just Javier's wallet, also the purple condom wrapper I held trapped beneath my thumb. It was sticking up, the ripped section jagged.

'What's that?' he asked.

Hurriedly I shoved the wallet and wrapper into my pocket. 'Nothing.'

'It is?'

'You should go.' I nodded up the corridor.

171

'Why are you holding a wallet and a condom wrapper?'

'I just found it, in there. I'm going to hand it in at reception so whoever lost it can pick it up.'

'You're going to hand in a condom wrapper?' There was incredulousness in his tone.

'Well, no, obviously not that, it can go in the bin.' I rolled my eyes. 'Someone has must been having a bit of down and dirty in the pharmacy on-call room. Probably Hartley and Emily.' I managed a strained laugh.

'No, I just left Hartley.' He narrowed his eyes. There was no humour in his expression.

'You really should go, Carl. Someone is probably dying because you're standing here, wondering about this stupid wrapper and wallet.'

He pushed his glasses into place. 'Who does the wallet belong to?'

'I don't know.'

'Just flick it open and look at the driving licence or something.'

'No, it's not my place to. I just found it. You should go.'

'Have a look.'

'No.'

'Why not?'

'Because I don't want to. Go, quickly.'

He squashed his lips together and after a quick look at the dark room behind me, ran off.

172

I stared at his retreating back. Bloody hell, why did it have to be Carl to come running around the corner at that moment? Just when I'd finally accepted that I wanted more with him, he found me holding a condom wrapper and Javier's wallet.

I sighed heavily as a hard lump of remorse landed in my belly. I'd kept my emotions suppressed for so long, not allowing myself to feel anything more than fondness for my friends-with-benefits, but now, tonight, the very moment I admitted that Carl was piercing my vulnerable core, the very centre of my soul, he discovered the real me.

And didn't like it.

I knew that for sure.

There had been something in his eyes, in that last glance. He'd seen the dark room and the wrapper. My uniform dishevelled, my hair ratty and my lipstick smudged.

Carl was a clever bloke, his IQ topping most people's. He'd guessed my secret. Well, half of it anyway. Yes, I'd been in there with a bloke, about to satisfy the craving he'd been stoking in me for weeks, but what he didn't know was I hadn't gone through with it.

I looked guilty as hell, but in actual fact I was completely innocent. Well, completely was maybe stretching it, but I was certainly more innocent than guilty.

I went back into the office. Flicked on the light and dropped on the sofa I'd been sprawled on minutes before

– sprawled on thinking of Carl and wishing it was him about to make love to me. I'd ruined my chance with the one bloke I'd cared about in years. He'd spend the next few hours with Javier and their sick patient. Javier was bound to notice his missing wallet at some point, comment, and Carl would put two and two together quicker than arterial blood hits the ceiling. Add in the wrapper, the room, my dishevelled state and his suspicions would be confirmed.

Carl would, by the end of the night, think that I was like every other dumb nurse in the hospital, desperate for a bit of Italian meat.

Well I wasn't. Javier didn't do it for me.

But it was too late. Carl would think that I was a slag, which I probably was in some people's eyes. That I just wanted to shag and not have a relationship, which, had anyone asked me last week, I would have agreed with. But now …

I tugged the wallet from my pocket. It was pale-brown leather with a football logo on the front, AC Milan. I flipped it open, wondering why it seemed so weighty. It must be full of wads of cash.

Immediately a smiling Javier grinned up at me. It was a photograph of him and a girl. She had long brunette hair held back from her face with large black sunglasses and was stunningly beautiful with dark eyes, wide red lips and smooth skin. They were leaning in close and cosy, behind them a dramatic backdrop of cliffs and then a perfect, deep-blue sea. He was holding her left hand out towards the camera. On her ring finger was a rock the size of a small island.

'You dirty rat,' I said. 'You've got an Italian beauty back home waiting for you and you mess around here like some kind of single agent.' I tutted and shook my head. 'Poor girl, whatever your name is. I'm afraid your fiancé isn't keeping his libido under even the tiniest whisper of control. You'd get more loyalty out of a starving tiger.'

I smoothed my finger over the small plastic window covering the picture, my heartstrings tugging that she was in love with such a player. She looked like a nice girl.

Suddenly I paused. There was something lumpy beneath the picture. Something hard, but flat. Curious, I poked my finger beneath. It was narrow and tight. I couldn't get at whatever it was.

Jesus, it was well tucked in, seriously well hidden. I pulled a pair of small clamping forceps from my pocket, the type I used to get stubborn, fiddly lids off cannulas. I manoeuvered and twiddled and finally got their little pointy ends into the space.

Another few seconds of manipulation and I had hold of whatever was secreted away behind Javier and his fiancée. Carefully I withdrew it.

A brass key.

Small, almost crudely cut. The pointy end that turned

the lock precise but the circle for holding it, attaching it to a key ring, was misshaped, there was no hole in it.

'What the …?' I held it up to the light. 'Why do you have a small, oddly shaped key in your wallet, Javier?'

It didn't look like a house key and definitely not a car key. It belonged to something little but lockable, a padlock, a shed maybe, or even a cycle lock. But why wouldn't he keep it on his key ring? Why was it separate and hidden?

Thoughts began to bombard me. Outrageous ideas. It couldn't be true. That was nuts!

I stood, clutching the key.

Sat again.

Stupid. Ludicrous. Absurd.

But I had to go and see.

I shoved the wallet back into my pocket and dashed from the office. Within seconds I was standing in front of the drug cupboard holding the key outstretched.

I didn't know why, because it wouldn't fit, I was sure of it. This peculiarly shaped, almost home-made-looking key would never work in this modern, metal cupboard. It was probably of sentimental value, his poor cheated-upon girlfriend had probably given it to him before he'd left for England – the key to her heart or something equally sappy.

'Go on,' I whispered and pushed it into the small hole. It slid in, smoothly, perfectly.

'OK, coincidence. It won't turn.'

Holding my breath and my heart thudding, I rotated the key.

There was a click and a squeak and the drug cupboard door popped open.

'Fucking hell.' Quickly I shut the door, re-turned the key and stepped back. Stared at the cupboard, the key, then the cupboard again.

Had I really solved Iceberg's mystery? It seemed I had. Doctor Javier Garelli was the drug thief.

But I needed evidence. I would never have thought Javier was the one taking the benzos, so why would she believe me when I told her?

I quickly opened the cupboard again, left the key in place with the doors ajar and whipped out my iPhone.

One click and I had my first piece of evidence.

I secured the cupboard, whizzed back into the pharmacy office and set the key next to his open wallet. Proof enough that it was his wallet because of the smiling photograph. My hands were shaking as I took another shot with my phone. Then I slipped the key halfway behind the smiling couple and snapped again.

Three pictures, all connecting Javier with the key and connecting the key with the drug cupboard. Proof enough for Iceberg and for Personnel to question him.

I slotted the key away, back into the same position I'd found it, and flipped the wallet shut.

The door opened.

'Javier,' I said, looking up.

His face was dark; he didn't wear his usual smile. 'My wallet,' he said, 'I dropped it.'

'Here.' I handed it over with a grin.

He snatched it from my grip. 'I hope you respected my privacy, Sharon.'

'It fell open on the floor, Javier, I couldn't help but look inside.' I paused. 'So I'm afraid I know your secret.'

There was a slight decrease in the colour in his cheeks. He curled his hands into fists. 'What secret?'

'But it's OK, I won't say anything.'

'I don't know what you mean. I have nothing to hide.' He pressed his lips together and pulled his eyebrows low. It occurred to me that he wasn't nearly as handsome when he wasn't smiling and getting his own way.

'Oh, but you do.'

He was silent, his breaths coming quick, his nostrils flaring slightly.

'Your girlfriend,' I said. 'I saw the picture. She is very beautiful.'

Still he said nothing.

'But don't worry. I have no intention of telling anyone that particular bit of information, Doctor Garelli. It's not worth my while.'

A muscle twitched in his cheek.

'So.' I stood and brushed my hands down my uniform,

178

slipped my phone away. 'I'm glad we didn't actually go all the way, because I've realised you're really not my type at all.'

'This girlfriend,' he said, making speech marks with his fingers. 'Is actually my sister. We were on a family holiday in Sorrento when that picture was taken.'

'Oh, you look very close.'

'We are twins.'

'Really?' What a load of rubbish.

'Yes, so go ahead and say what you want. No one will believe you.'

'You don't think so?'

'No, especially when I tell them I rejected you and that is why you are spreading malicious rumours about me.'

Bloody hell, he really did turn off the charm like a switch. Rachael's words came back to me about his mood swings. Was that his natural disposition or was it benzos that made him this way?

'You do whatever you feel you need to,' I said, pushing past him. 'And I will do what I feel is the right thing to do too.'

I walked up the corridor, speedily, hoping he wouldn't follow me.

He didn't, and within a couple of minutes I was heading up the backstairs towards Iceberg's office. My head was spinning but my thoughts were clearing steadily.

Chapter Seven

I knocked on Iceberg's office door.

'Come in.'

Good, she was there. The sooner I sorted out this damn mess once and for all, the better.

'Ah, Sharon,' she said, 'I trust you have information if you're here and not skulking around pharmacy.'

'Actually, I have.'

She raised her eyebrows. 'Well, sit down then.'

I did as she'd asked, a bubble of excitement growing within me. Not only was I going to get the pleasure of revealing the thief and getting myself off the hook, I was also going to be treated to the satisfaction of seeing her face, when the guy she was smitten with, turned out to be the culprit.

'Oh, before I forget, this has been sitting on my desk for you.' Iceberg shoved forward a plain white envelope. 'And I would appreciated it if you didn't use the hospital for your private correspondence, we're not here for your convenience, you know.'

I took the letter, glanced at my name written neatly on the front and addressed simply to care of the senior night nurse. 'Er, thanks. I don't know who –'

'So spit it out,' she said, leaning forward on the desk, her fingers tapping on a brown file. 'What have you discovered?'

I sucked in a deep breath and folded the letter into my pocket. 'I found a key, a small, brass key that looks to me as though it's been very carefully, but roughly cut. Perhaps with hand tools rather than a machine.'

'And ...' She gnawed on the inside of her cheek.

'And the key unlocks the drug cupboard the temazepam has been going missing from.'

'Really?' She widened her eyes, almost smiled. 'So, who had this key?'

'Has, still has it. After I discovered it, I tested it was the one we were looking for then secretly replaced it.'

'Bloody hell, how did you do that?'

'The person in question was, shall we say, rather distracted throughout the whole event.' I waggled my eyebrows suggestively.

'Ah, so it's a man and you've used your womanly ways to trick him.' If she wasn't such a cow I'd have almost thought her expression was approving.

'That is one way of describing it.'

'So tell me, put me out of my misery. Then I can call Personnel first thing and clear this whole scandalous matter up.'

I paused, savouring the moment. His thieving name was on my lips, tingling my tongue. She was going to flip and I didn't care one bit, she needed to start seeing people for what they were. Sorting out the good from the bad, the wheat from the chaff. It was clearly something she had a problem with.

'The key belongs to Doctor Javier Garelli.'

'No.' She gasped. 'You're lying.'

I shook my head. 'Nope, it is true.'

'It's ridiculous, Doctor Garelli isn't taking benzodiazepines. If he was he wouldn't be able to work as a very skilled, incredibly talented surgeon, saving countless lives.'

I shrugged. 'In all fairness, how well is he functioning?'

'How dare you be so impudent about one of your seniors.' She stood, balled her fists on the table and leant forward, reminding me of a gorilla about to charge.

'I'm not being impudent,' I said calmly, 'I'm merely stating facts. He's been operating, yes, but Doctor Carl Rogers told me he was the one that managed to get an awkward foreign object from a patient's rectum the other day, Javier just couldn't do it. And only tonight they were having major problems with a hemi-colectomy. Perhaps Javier's skills are not all they should be.'

'Preposterous.' Her cheeks were reddening, and her eyes flashed with anger.

'And you have to admit, he can be pretty moody,' I added.

'Not that I've seen. He's always the epitome of charm.'

'Well, it's one of the things I've heard on my hunt for gossip, at your request, I hasten to add. His moods blow hot and cold and he's got a history of sleeping issues, which could have easily been why he started helping himself to the temazepam in the first place.'

'He could have just got a prescription from his own doctor.'

'In the short term, yes, but my guess is he got dependent, or started taking it recreationally and had to boost his supplies.'

'Nonsense.' She pointed her finger at me and set her jaw at a hard, mean angle. 'You are a lying, manipulative bitch, Nurse Roane, and for some reason you've decided to try and ruin a good and decent man's career.' She straightened, narrowed her eyes and nodded. 'And I know exactly why!'

'You do?'

'Yes, you've got the hots for him and he's obviously turned you down. I saw the way you were dribbling over him in Accident and Emergency the other night. God, it made me feel sick to see you with that stupid lovesick expression on your face and all giggly and pathetic.'

'I can assure you that isn't the case, I –'

'So you tried to drop your knickers for him in some sleazy corner and he refused you.' She folded her arms. 'And now you're angry with him for the rejection.'

183

'I'm not angry at him at all, and it's Javier Garelli we're talking about, does he ever refuse a shag?'

'Like any decent man he does when he's in a relationship, and the fact that he turned you down just proves his loyal, upstanding nature.'

'He's in a relationship?' I asked. Did she know about the Italian beauty? No, surely not.

'Yes, as a matter of fact he is.'

'Who with?'

'That's none of your business.'

I leant back on the chair and folded my arms. Oh, my God. This was hysterical, Iceberg was actually referring to herself. She really did think she was in a relationship with him. 'Oh, you must mean the girl he has a picture of in his wallet. The glamorous one with the red lips and the giant diamond on her finger?'

She sucked in a sharp breath. 'What?'

'Yes, his fiancée back in Italy. Everyone knows about her, she's waiting faithfully for him to go back and marry her when he's completed his registrar placement.' OK, so I was making some stuff up now, but I was on a roll. Watching the colour drain from Iceberg's face was such a treat. 'She's a stunner. I'm not surprised he's staying faithful to her. They will have beautiful children that's for sure.'

'You're lying.'

'I'm not. I've seen the picture and the key. It's all true.'

'Get out.'

'What?'

'Get out. I have something to do, someone I need to speak to ...'

Good. She'd finally come to her senses. I wouldn't like to be Javier when she got hold of him. She looked ready to explode and that would be a messy and unpleasant sight. 'Doctor Garelli is on call. I suspect he's on Eyre Ward with his post-op if you want to go straight there.'

'No, you stupid nurse. I need to speak to Personnel right this instant. I don't care if it's the middle of the night this has to be handled properly.'

'Good idea, let them approach him, with security. You don't know what he might do when he realises that his means for helping himself to temazepam has been discovered.'

'I don't need to talk to Personnel about Javier,' she spat. 'I need to speak to them about you. Clearly you're mentally unstable and too emotionally unfit to be working in this hospital.'

'Me?' Shock railroaded my body, making me catch my breath and causing my vision to blur.

'Yes, you. I don't want you registered as an employee of this hospital for any longer than is absolutely necessary and I intend for your contract to be terminated before the sun comes up. With no notice, obviously.'

'You can't do that.' My mouth was suddenly dry, my

throat tight. Lose my job, here, now! Just when I thought I'd solved my problems.

'Of course I can, because you, Nurse Roane, are responsible for an act of gross misconduct last week. And you don't deserve to continue nursing for another moment.'

'But, but you said you wouldn't report that if I found out who was stealing from the drug cupboard.'

'Yes, but all you've done is lie. You've made something up about a perfect gentleman in order to get yourself off the hook. I can't and won't stand for it. Do you seriously think I'll allow his long, arduous medical training to be thrown away by a malicious rumour? Think of all the lives he has yet to save with his skilled hands. Do you really want the murder of all those people on your conscience?'

Jesus, she was the mad one in the room. 'What about all the patients he might kill because he's not functioning properly, because he's coming down from a high or due his next one?'

'I will not discuss this with you any further. Remove yourself from hospital premises. You're relieved of all your duties as of now. Expect a call from the head of Personnel first thing in the morning to confirm your termination.'

I stood, my legs weak, my heart thumping. I should have guessed that she wouldn't keep her side of the bargain. Bitch. I did exactly what she'd asked, even when I thought she'd set me an impossible task, and still she was going to throw me to the lions. 'I'll go,' I said, 'because

I can't stand to be in a hospital where the senior nurse can't see what's going on beneath her nose.'

Her lips tightened.

'You should try and think back,' I went on. 'To when he had you over a table in out-patients. Did you misplace your keys for a while afterwards? Did he steal them from you in the throes of passion and then take a mould of the one he wanted in clay or soap or something, only to carve out a replica later?'

'How dare you!'

'You should try and rack your brains, because you're the only one outside of pharmacy with that key. If you allowed him to get close to you, then perhaps he took advantage and made a copy of it for himself.'

I was going to add that it was likely the only reason he went anywhere near her, but the look on her face was dire. She was red and blotchy, her eyes moist but flashing. Her chest rising and falling rapidly and her hands shaking.

We stared at each other. The air sizzled with tension, and in that moment I knew that Javier had indeed screwed her solely to get that key. Slimy bastard. Thank goodness I hadn't gone through with my plan to get up close and personal with him. Yuk, just the thought of it.

'Get out,' she spat. 'Now.'

I stood and went for the door. I thought she might hurl more abuse at me, but she didn't. She was silent. No doubt a whole pile of pennies were dropping in her brain. She'd come to see the truth, once she'd calmed down. The facts were there, on the table the same way she'd been.

Damn, the pictures on my iPhone. I'd forgotten to show them to her. She would have to believe me then. I turned. 'I have evidence. If you give me your mobile number I can send you pictures.'

'What the hell are you talking about?'

'I have three pictures, of the key.'

She swallowed, sat back heavily on her chair and absently recited a string of numbers from memory. Hurriedly I tapped them into my phone then hit send on the damning photographs.

Her mobile beeped from her handbag on the floor by the desk. She picked it up, rummaged, then slid her finger over the screen, checking out the pictures.

'Really?' she said scornfully. 'Is this it?'

'Yes, that's the key in the cupboard and the key in his wallet. You can tell it's his wallet because of the picture of him and his fiancée.'

She was staring at it, unblinking. 'This means nothing.'

'What?' I stepped forward. 'It's proof, and certainly evidence enough for him to be questioned, by Personnel and the police.'

'A feeble attempt at slander,' she said, shaking her head. 'These pictures are useless and clearly completely fabricated.'

'But the door, to the cupboard. It's open, with the key. The key from his wallet.'

'A blurred, dark, barely discernible photograph of a cupboard. A picture of a photograph with a key. Hardly evidence, Nurse Roane. Now please, get out and don't come back. Just go home and wait for the final details of your termination. Expect it to be swift and to the point, sexual relations with a patient being a particularly clear cut reason for getting rid of you.'

I couldn't believe what she was saying. My brain heard the words but I could hardly process them. The pictures were absolute confirmation of everything I'd said. Why the hell would I make them up? Create them? That would make no sense at all.

I turned and left the office, my feet heavy, my legs weak and a bit shaky. There was no point trying to argue or reason with Iceberg. She was a power-crazy, irrational bitch who was a complete sucker for a handsome man. She was also a cold-hearted cow when it came to compassion. She believed what she wanted to believe and there was nothing I could do about it.

Damn shame my fate was in her hands. No, it was more than a shame, it was bloody catastrophic.

I cycled home in the dark and the rain. By the time I let myself into my flat it was nearly five o'clock in the morning and I was drenched. The few cars that were out had all splashed me as they'd whizzed past, the drivers clearly surprised to see a dead-of-the-night cyclist on the quiet roads.

The flat was cold, so I flicked on the heating then stripped and stepped into a hot shower. May as well make the most of such luxuries. When I was living on the streets in a few months' time, I'd miss them.

I held my face to the steaming water. What the hell had I done to deserve Iceberg in my life? I'd had a hundred different senior nurses over the years in various departments, but none as pure evil as her. None that would have treated me the way she had for my step out of line.

Nurses were nurses because they cared passionately about the well-being of other human beings. So why the hell was Iceberg a nurse? What had called her into the profession? She didn't have a compassionate, empathetic, nurturing bone in her body. She was a look-after-number-one person. I supposed it was just as well she was in a management role and kept away from actual sick people. Likely she would finish them off. One stony look from her and they'd lose the will to live.

I lathered my body in strawberry shower-gel. It smelt extra nice, possibly because soon I'd have that manky, damp, rotten-feet smell all tramps have. Trampy Sharon, that would be me, and not trampy in a sleeping around way, but in a dirty, fleabag, bottle-of-whiskey-clutched-in-my-fingerless-gloved-hands way.

It wasn't a pleasant future to look forward to.

Eventually I forced myself out of the shower, dressed in fluffy pink pyjamas with matching slippers and poured myself a glass of white wine. I knew I should have some dinner, something nutritious, but I didn't trust whatever I made to stay down. My stomach felt twisted and tight, like it was a scrunched up ball, and my throat was narrow and dry. I wasn't sure if I tried to swallow anything would go down. It would just sit there, like a chunk of cardboard and make me gag.

Gulping wine, which went down well enough, I flicked on the TV. Breakfast news was just starting its first of many round-ups of the country's events. Widespread flooding in the Lake District was the leading story running with images of murky water siphoning between two rows of terraced houses, and the firemen rowing a family of four to safety down Kendal High Street.

Perhaps I'd knock Kendal off my list of possible towns to be homeless in, though I was rather partial to the mint cake there. Maybe the tourists would hand it out to beggars.

A sudden gust of wind accompanied by a loud splattering of rain hit the window. I shuddered, glad that I was home in the dry, for now at least. My flat was on the top floor, there were only five beneath me, but still it meant it caught the weather. When Michael and I had bought the place years ago I'd liked it, hearing the elements when we were cosy indoors, snuggled up on the sofa. But then when he'd left it had just reminded me of my aloneness. I'd felt like my own star in a *Wuthering Heights* style drama, me against the world and hiding the madness that had gone hand in hand with my heartbreak.

As I'd got used to single life, though, it suited me again, the wind and rain, hailstones even. It was all part of Yorkshire's rich weather system and my love of the county was one of the reasons I'd stayed when I could have upped and travelled the world.

That would never happen now. No nursing qualification equalled no global ticket to work and travel.

I finished my glass of wine as the news story loop began again, and reached for the remote, intent on finding some soap catch-ups to watch. There was no point trying to sleep, my head was a cacophony of trials and tribulations, there was no chance exhaustion would be kind and take me away from it all. It was better to sit and stare at the box.

The intercom system rang from the hallway. A determined buzz.

What the? Six o'clock in the morning. Who could that be?

Quickly, I went to the hall and pressed the buzzer. 'Yes?'

'Sharon, it's me. Can I come in? It's bloody horrible out here.'

'Carl?'

'Yes, open the damn door. I need to talk to you.'

Damn. What did he want to talk about? Was he mad as hell at me? Had Javier confirmed his suspicions even though they weren't true?

I worried at my bottom lip and hovered my finger over the door switch. I hadn't even begun to unravel my feelings for Carl since the whole Javier-condom wrapper affair. My world crashing down had taken up my thoughts. But those feelings were there. Remorse, guilt, anger and also just a thin sliver of that wonderful epiphany when I'd realised my heart and body wanted Carl and no one else. And not just for sex but for him, I really felt we could –

The bell buzzed again, long and insistent. Bugger, that would wake the neighbours. There'd be hell to pay if that happened. Still, they wouldn't have to put up with me for much longer.

Hurriedly, I pressed the switch to let him in and stared at my reflection in the hall mirror. My hair was a mess, I'd only towel-dried it after my shower. My face was a little shiny from night cream, and my pink pyjamas, though snuggly and warm, were probably my least seductive item of clothing. Also I was clutching an empty wine glass so tight I began to wonder why the stem hadn't broken.

There was a knock on the flat door. He'd been fast,

probably taken the stairs rather than the slow, rattling elevator.

'Carl,' I said as I opened the door. 'What are you doing here?'

He stood before me panting and damp, but not soaked. Droplets of water balanced in his windswept hair and dotted the lenses of his glasses. His cheeks were a little red and his black leather jacket shiny with rain.

He looked at me. Like he was seeing me for the first time. Briefly, I wondered if it was because of my overdose on pink and absolute lack of glamour, but then I realised that it was something else.

The twist in my gut intensified as I wondered just what the hell Javier had said to him. Goodness knew what twaddle had come out of his Italian mouth.

'I brought food,' Carl said, holding up a brown McDonald's bag. 'And coffee.'

'I'm on the wine.'

'It's morning.' He raised his eyebrows.

'Not when you're permanently nocturnal it's not. This is my evening.' I turned and wandered into the kitchen. If he had something to say he could just say it. I wasn't going to drag it out of him.

The front door clicked shut and I heard him shrug out of his jacket and follow me. I poured wine then glanced at him standing in the doorway of the kitchen. He had to stoop otherwise the top of his head would have touched the frame. He'd removed his shoes.

'You want a glass?' I asked.

He glanced at his watch. 'Well, I'm officially off duty.' He paused. 'Go on then, never had wine with a McDonald's breakfast before, but there you go.'

I filled a glass for him, placing it on the counter near the door. 'So what do you need to talk about?'

'Eat first,' he said.

'I'm not hungry.'

'But you've been at work all night.'

'Well, obviously I haven't been at work all night, otherwise I would still be there.'

'I noticed your bike gone. Wondered if you'd come home ill.'

'No, I'm quite well.'

Why was he being so nice? Why wasn't he shouting at me for getting naked with Javier? Did he think I was such an easy lay that it wasn't worth discussing? It was just what he expected of me?

What had I become?

I pushed past him, into the living room.

'Sharon.' He gripped my upper arm. 'Talk to me.'

'You said you wanted to talk to me, remember?' I couldn't keep the irritation from my voice.

'I do, we have some things to set straight.'

'Such as?'

'Javier Garelli would be a good starting point.'

OK, so there it was, out in the open. I swallowed and dragged in a breath. Braced for the onslaught. 'What about him?'

'You know I like you, a lot, I've told you that, but earlier ...' A flash of pain crossed his eyes and it was like I was suddenly kicked in the shins. Damn it, I'd put that pain there. Sweet Carl, who didn't deserve to be hurt.

'Earlier,' he went on. 'When I was running to the crash call, you, he ... you'd been together, hadn't you?'

I looked away. Unable to hold his stare.

'Please, answer me,' he said quietly.

'Why, does it matter?'

He shook his head. 'It matters because I'd got some foolish idea in my head that we had something going on.' He paused. 'That you wanted me. But then you hooked up with him for a quickie at our very first stumble.'

'It's not like that.' I shrugged my arm. 'You don't understand.'

He released me and I sat at the small dining table in the corner of the living room. Nursed my wine and stared at a photograph of my childhood dog, Tinker, which hung on the wall.

He took a seat opposite, setting his wine and the McDonald's bag between us. 'So make me understand.'

'Why are you even here, Carl? If you think I fucked Javier when we had something going? Why are you here, pestering me about it?'

196

He flinched.

I sighed. 'I'm sorry, I'm kind of out of practise at the whole relationship thing.'

'But not with the shag buddies thing?'

'A girl has needs.'

'So you couldn't wait for me to attend to those needs, next Saturday, after dinner, like I said I would?'

'Last Friday would have suited me perfectly well.' I shoved my hand through my hair, tried to fluff it a little then sighed when it flopped limply around my ears. 'I thought there was something between us too, Carl. But I suppose you can't move beyond the Javier incident.'

He reached out, covering my hand with his. 'If that was the case I wouldn't be here, would I?'

My stomach clenched, my throat clogged. He was still here even though he really did believe that Javier and I had been down and dirty in the on-call room. 'Do you mean that?'

'Sharon, believe me, the thought of Javier or anyone else touching you makes me feel sick to my stomach. But I still like you, I still … want you.'

I sipped my wine, struggling to swallow the icy liquid. When it had finally gone down I spoke, 'I didn't, with Javier earlier, or in fact on any night, or would ever in the future.'

He closed his eyes for a good two or three seconds then blew out a long, slow breath. 'OK.'

'What you saw was a mistake.'

'A mistake?'

'Yes, I was going to – you've had me thinking about sex so damn much, and with all your Victorian ideas of chivalry I was just about ready to combust. So when Javier offered it on a plate I thought, sod it, a bit of nookie might just take the edge off it.'

He released my hand and took a big gulp of his wine. 'So the condom wrapper had been … he'd got that far?'

'Yes, and then the emergency bleep went off and he scarpered.'

'Thank God for Mr Singh's lousy clotting.'

'Is he OK?'

'Transferred to the intensive care unit, Javier should never have passed him for surgery in the first place. Hartley is up in arms about it.'

Yet another slip-up. How many more till he put someone six feet under? 'That's interesting.'

'Why?' He tilted his head.

'I don't know what you think of me, Carl, but I actually wasn't hanging around pharmacy hoping to spread my legs for Javier. Iceberg had given me a secret mission.'

'Sounds intriguing.'

I nodded. 'Eat your breakfast, it's going cold.'

He reached for the bag and began to pull out various items. 'You want some?'

'No.'

He frowned a little but didn't press the issue. 'So, are you going to start from the beginning?'

'The beginning, mmm ...' I sipped my wine. Where to start? Definitely not with Ted's handjob, that wouldn't go down well, not when Carl was handling my liaison with Javier so well. The story of a spur-of-the-moment wank for a helpless patient might just put him off his breakfast. Tip the balance of calm sanity to horrified rage.

'Iceberg has never liked me,' I said, 'she's always threatening to report me to Personnel for ridiculous misdemeanours, like sitting down instead of cleaning out cupboards when it's quiet, or taking too long on my break. She's such a cow, I hate her.'

'Doesn't everyone?' He munched into a hash brown.

'Yes, absolutely. Except, that is, for Javier.'

'What?' He raised his eyebrows.

I raised mine and nodded.

He looked shocked. 'Javier and Iceberg are an item? Don't be ridiculous.'

I managed a twisted smile. 'Ridiculous, yes, but it's not what you think. Iceberg has been having a problem with temazepam going missing from the night stock cupboard outside pharmacy. She's the only one with a key, legitimately anyway, but someone has been regularly helping themselves.'

'Probably someone from pharmacy. Making a bit of cash on the side by selling onto the street.'

'No, the hospital did a big investigation into that. Not possible. It was someone else with a key, someone working in the hospital at night.'

'But temazepam is generally used as night sedation, why would a night worker take it? They need to stay awake.'

I rolled my eyes. 'Night staff who rotate to days are notorious for having trouble sleeping. Their circadian rhythms are all over the place. That's why I stick to nights and nothing else. I'm in that routine now and it suits.'

'So someone was taking temazepam to sleep in the day?'

'Yes, initially I suspect that was the reason. But users become addicted, don't they? It's supposed to be for short-term use but if it's used in the long term you get hooked. Plus it does give a very lovely high.'

'So I've heard, but it's easy to become tolerant to it.'

'Meaning you need more and more.'

'I suppose so.' He nodded.

'Which was why someone had gone to extreme lengths to get their hands on it.' I took a mouthful of wine, warming to my story. 'So anyway, Iceberg set me a task of finding out who had this other key. I wanted to bang my head against a brick wall. It was like trying to find a needle in a haystack, literally. She'd been getting more and more impatient for me to feed her information and tonight, she ordered me to hang out by the cupboard and see if anyone came along and dipped into it. Well, you can imagine I wasn't very impressed with this assignment, but what choice did I have?

'So I was lurking around when suddenly Javier appears behind me. He was his usual suave self and before I knew it he was smooth-talking me into the pharmacy on-call room and rolling on a condom.'

Carl put his hash brown back in its wrapper. Took a swig of wine and pressed his lips together. He appeared to be struggling to swallow. 'What does this bit have to do with the missing drugs?' he managed.

'Everything.' I hesitated. 'We were just about to, you know, and I told him to stop –'

'Why?'

'Because.' I paused as those feelings of need for Carl and only Carl resurfaced. 'I suddenly realised, that despite Javier's charm and good looks, which for the record I don't believe in any more, I really didn't want him.' I took a fast sip of wine. 'I didn't want to shag him or anyone else. It was like a cartoon, you know, when a light bulb goes off over a character's head and they get an idea, or an epiphany; that's what happened to me.'

Carl was silent for a long moment, then, 'And what was this epiphany?'

I rubbed my fingers over my brow and then in a circle at my temple. 'I suddenly realised that I wanted to make love, not fuck. That just the physical act of sex wasn't enough for me any more. I was ready to move on and undo some of the bolts I'd put around my heart.' Hesitantly I looked him in the eye. I'd laid my soul bare to him. Would he accept it, laugh at me or be disgusted?

He creased his brow. 'What the hell did some bastard do to you, Sharon?'

'I'll tell you another time.' I rolled my eyes, trying to act as though it had been nothing, even though it had been devastating. 'So anyway, I came to a swift realisation that I was ready for connection again and it most definitely wasn't Javier that I wanted to hook up with. So I told him to stop, several times. He was pretty insistent and he's a big, heavy guy. I was just starting to panic that I couldn't push him off even though I was kicking and shoving and –'

'Bastard,' Carl spat. His fists clenched on the table as he pushed the remains of his breakfast to one side. 'I should go and fucking deck the Italian piece of –'

'No. I told you, nothing happened, and I'm certain he would have got the message in another few seconds, but suddenly it was over. His pager went off and he dashed out of the room and up the corridor. That was just seconds before I saw you.'

Carl's expression was still grim but his fists relaxed a little.

'And that was when I found it.'

'What?'

202

'The key, to the drug cupboard.'

'What?'

'The key, to the drug cupboard, it was in Javier's wallet.'

'Jesus. No way!'

'Yes way. I flipped it open, saw a picture of him and his fiancée –'

'Fiancée, what a dirty rat. He's the biggest tart in the hospital.' Carl was shaking his head in amazement.

'My thoughts exactly, and it was behind that picture I found a key. It was a bit rough but it worked in the cupboard just fine.'

'Jesus Christ.' Carl sat back, pushed his hand through his hair making it stick up messily. 'You have to tell someone about this. He's not fit to be working if he's abusing benzodiazepines. Bloody hell, he's been operating half the night.'

'I've already tried to report him. I went straight to Iceberg, but she wouldn't believe me. She thinks the sun shines out of his arse. Said I was just trying to discredit him. She told me to go home and expect a phone call from Personnel to tell me that I'm sacked.'

'What? You haven't done anything wrong. She can't do that?'

'It seems she can.'

'But there are laws, unions, contracts, things to protect you when you're innocent.'

I shrugged and drained my wine. There were indeed laws to protect employees, but not if those employees had broken codes of conduct. But I couldn't tell Carl that.

'So that's what I'm doing now,' I said. 'Waiting for my P45 while Javier goes home, takes some of the pills he's been nicking and has a nice little trip at my expense.'

'I should go to the medical board or Hartley or something.' He tapped his knuckles on his chin. 'Trouble is, there isn't any evidence.'

'I put the key back in his wallet, but not until I'd taken some pictures of it on my iPhone.'

'Brilliant.' His face lit. 'That's great.'

'Not really. I showed Iceberg and she said they were crap quality and it looked like I'd fabricated them.'

'But why would she think that?'

'I told you, she's hot for him, thinks they're in a "relationship".' I made quote marks with my fingers.

'She's hardly his type.' Carl looked bemused.

'Well, she thinks she is, and I suppose he does too, if by shagging her it meant he got his hands on her keys, amongst other things.'

'Bloody hell, Sharon. I can't believe you've had all this going on.'

'It's been a nightmare that has turned into a disaster. God knows what I'm going to do when I can't pay the mortgage on this place next month. I was only just making ends meet as it was. We bought this on two salaries.'

'We?' He tipped his head.

I glanced down at my ring finger. A ruby set in white gold had once sat there. Now it lived in my jewellery box. 'Michael,' I said. 'We bought it together not long after we got engaged.'

'You were engaged?' There was surprise in his voice.

'Yes, for a year.'

'What happened?'

My mobile trilled to life saving me from talking of a past best left buried.

'I should get that,' I said, reaching it from my handbag that was looped over the back of the chair. It was a hospital number. My heart rate picked up a notch and it had already been going pretty fast.

'Hello.'

'Is that Sharon Roane?'

'Yes.'

'Hello, this is Felicity Broom from Personnel. I'm sorry to be calling so early but I've just had a rather strange call from Sister Stanton about you.'

'Strange?' I glanced at Carl. He was unwrapping his McMuffin.

'Yes, she seems to think you've been having some kind of sexual relationship with a gentleman patient.'

Bitch, she'd gone ahead and reported me. 'Well that's ridiculous. Utterly ridiculous.' Denial seemed the best angle to adopt at this point.

'Well, it is rather an unusual situation, especially as it isn't the patient who has brought the incident to our attention.'

'I don't even know what patient you're referring to,' I said.

'You don't?'

'No. I work on a different ward every night, I'm bank staff.'

'Oh, yes, I see. Well I'm afraid Sister Stanton wants to take this matter further.'

'Tell them,' Carl said, frowning. 'About Javier.' He bit into his bun.

'What do you mean by further?'

'She wants you to be suspended and for a formal inquiry to be held.'

Just suspended. I supposed that was better than sacked, for now. 'Can she do that if there hasn't been a patient complaint?'

'Well, it seems she can. Though like I said, it is rather unusual.'

'So no patient, nor a family member or any other staff have an issue with me; it's just her word against mine.'

'Well, yes, I suppose it is.'

'Well it's an outlandish accusation and I completely deny it.'

I looked at Carl and shrugged, widening my eyes as though I didn't know what the hell was going on.

206

'Well, I, yes, it is rather untoward, and given that it is a burn victim, the whole idea is really incredibly unsavoury.'

'I couldn't agree more.'

'Go on,' Carl said, nodding. 'Tell her.'

I nodded and mouthed 'hang on', then returned my attention to Felicity Broom. 'But I did think I might be subjected to a ridiculous, untrue allegation,' I said slowly.

'You did?' She sounded surprised. 'Why?'

'Because I reported an incident to Sister Stanton earlier on tonight and she didn't believe me. In fact, she accused me of lying and said she would try to discredit me by any means possible.'

She hesitated, then, 'Go on.'

'The missing benzodiazepines from the pharmacy night cupboard. I know who's been taking them.'

She gave a sharp intake of breath. 'You do?'

'Yes.'

'Who?'

I paused for a little dramatic effect, and then said, 'Doctor Javier Garelli.'

'No? Really? The hunky Italian one?'

I rolled my eyes and sighed. 'Yeah, that's the one.'

'How on earth do you know that?'

'I found a key, in his wallet. It opens the drug cupboard. Plus I know he's not been on the ball lately. There's something going on with him. Nurses and doctors are talking about his mood swings and his mistakes.'

'Bloody hell, this situation has been a nightmare for the last few months, the police have been involved and everything.'

'Well, if you take a look in his wallet, under the photo there, you'll find a replica key to Sister Stanton's, and my betting is, he took it from her and made a copy for himself.'

'But hospital keys are coded. Hardware shops are not allowed to replicate them, by law.'

'I know, but this one looks handcrafted, crudely yes, but it works.'

She paused. 'Sharon, if what you're saying is true this is quite a breakthrough.'

'It is true.' I felt like I was floating. She believed me. Thank goodness. 'I have evidence. Photographs I took with my iPhone that Sister Stanton said I'd faked. Would you like me to get them to you?'

'Yes. Definitely. If you send them through to this number that would be great. Then I'll have a word with my superior and call you back. But thanks, this is incredible. You've done the hospital a great service.'

'So I'm not suspended or sacked?'

'I do need to speak to my superior before I can comment on that. Like I said, this is a very unusual situation and I really can't see why Sister Stanton didn't mention your discoveries to us.'

'She just flatly refused to believe me.'

'Mmm, Sharon, I'll call you back soon.'

'OK.' I clicked off the phone and began to forward the three photographs.

'Well?' Carl asked, glancing at the screen.

'She needs to speak to her superior; then she's going to call back.'

'So this means you're off the hook with Iceberg?'

I laughed, but not with much humour. 'The way my life is going, Carl, I very much doubt it. Things just don't seem to be working out very well.'

'Hey.' He stood and moved to sit in the chair next to mine. 'Am I included in the not-working-out bracket?'

He looked tired. There were rings under his eyes again. His stubble was dense and his collar undone; he hadn't bothered with a tie when changing from his scrubs.

'I suppose so.'

He tucked a strand of hair behind my ear. 'Why?'

'Because the last thing I wanted was for you to see me with Javier, for there to ever have even been an incident with Javier. But it happened, and it was wrong and –'

Suddenly he pressed his lips to mine, a soft but firm kiss, and I couldn't utter another word. A whimper escaped my mouth as his hand slid to the back of my head, cradled my skull, and his tongue sought mine.

After a few delicious moments he pulled away, but he didn't let go of my head. 'So let's just start over. No games, no one else, just us.'

His glasses were always a little askew after he'd kissed

me and I reached up and straightened them. 'OK, if that's what you want?'

'Yes, most definitely. I thought nurses were easy but you've been quite a challenge, in every department.'

'Easy! How dare you!'

He laughed. 'It's why I became a doctor in the first place. For the nurses.'

'I can't believe you had the nerve to say that.'

He laughed harder and dragged me into a tight hug. 'Luckily I like a challenge, though. And you definitely come under that heading.'

I melted into him. For the first time in days, weeks, months, I felt safe and secure. Carl's arms were like coming home. Warm and comforting. And his unique, fresh, masculine smell had also become reassuring.

I slid my hands up his back; taut with trim muscle over wide shoulders. I just liked touching him and having him hold me. If he didn't want to take it any further for now then that was fine with me.

He kissed the side of my head, stroked my hair then ran his finger over my cheek. Another little piece of my heart melted for him. Such a simple gesture, but weighted with kindness, despite what I must have put his emotions through half of the night.

'So when you had this sudden light bulb moment,' he said, 'and realised that you wanted to make love. Was it anything to do with me?'

I looked up at his anxious face. 'Do you even have to ask?' I touched the tip of my nose to his and enjoyed the sensation of being honest and open, not just to myself about my feelings but also to Carl. It was something I hadn't done for so long. Emotions I'd learnt could break you as easily as they could make you. But with Carl, well, he was worth the risk of feeling again.

My phone suddenly jangled out its tinny tune. Hurriedly I reached for it. Carl kept an arm around my shoulders and I rested my hand on his thigh.

'Hello.'

'Sharon?'

'Yes.'

'It's Felicity Broom again.'

'Any news?'

'Yes, I've spoken to the head of Personnel who is most shocked that Sister Stanton didn't think your accusation and evidence was worth sharing with us and the police. It really is very inappropriate for a manager in her position and certainly will require an investigation of its own.'

'Really?' Oh, hell. How sweet was that? Iceberg in trouble for not passing on my information. A double whammy of success. 'And Javier?'

'I can't say much more, because a very current investigation is taking place.'

Bloody hell, did that mean the police were on their way to raid his place? I hoped so. I could just imagine his handsome face twisting with fury that they dare accuse him, Doctor Javier Garelli. He would likely implode with rage. 'Oh, OK then.'

'But we really are incredibly grateful for your investigative skills and for feeling able to report a superior. It takes a lot of courage to do that.'

'Well, I'm not one to see many grey areas between right and wrong.'

'And a good job, too, because both of these members of staff are most definitely in the wrong.'

Both. Excellent. 'You know they're having an affair, don't you?' I said.

Carl gave a shocked cough then cleared his throat.

'Really?' Felicity said, her voice high with surprise.

'Yes, so that might be why Sister Stanton felt the need to protect him like she did.'

'Well, yes, that would certainly explain some things.' She paused. 'Really, those two?'

'Hard to believe but it's common knowledge.'

'Well, I would never have guessed, they don't seem exactly ...'

'Suited? No I agree.'

'Mmm.'

'So,' I said. 'Can I ask what will happen about my suspension?'

'Oh, yes that. Forget it, obviously. Sister Stanton will be the one suspended now, for not reporting Doctor Garelli.'

'And the thing she accused me of?' I glanced at Carl who was finishing off the last of his McMuffin.

'Water under the bridge. Clearly she's been having trouble distinguishing between the good guys and the bad guys as well as reality.'

I was off the hook. I wanted to do a hop, skip and a jump. Iceberg had failed to strike me off the register. I was still a nurse, always would be. Thank goodness, because it was all I really knew how to do.

'Great,' I said, trying to sound relieved more than jubilant. 'Good.'

'Yes, forget it all. We'll be in touch if we need anything else from you, but I doubt it. These pictures are pretty damning, and once the police have done their investigation, too, it should be a closed case.'

'So I can turn up for duty as normal.'

'Yes, absolutely. The hospital is lucky to have you.'

I let out a long breath of relief. She couldn't have said a nicer thing to me. 'I'd best get some sleep then, it's been a long night.'

Chapter Eight

'All sorted?' Carl asked as I slotted my phone back into my handbag.

'Yes, yes it is. I've gone from thinking I was about to be made homeless and living as a tramp on the streets to being thanked by Personnel and told the hospital is lucky to have me.' I shook my head, hardly able to believe my turnaround in fortune.

'Well, yes, they are lucky to have you, but I don't think you would ever have been on the streets,' he said.

'Where else would I go, if I lost this place?' I genuinely had no idea. I would be desolate.

'My house?'

'You've got a house? I thought you said you were in the doctors' accommodation at the hospital.'

'I was, but I figured I'd be hanging around for a few years and I wanted to get on the property ladder, so I've just put an offer in on a little place. You should come over when I move in, it's cute. Thatched roof, apple trees

214

in the back garden and a fabulous wood-burning stove, perfect for cold winter nights.' He stood and pulled me up next to him. 'You would never have been living on the street, not when I'm on this earth.'

'Really?' A sudden set of tears welled in my eyes. 'That's so kind.'

'Hey, hey.' He rubbed his thumbs beneath my eyes, catching the drips before they trickled down my cheeks. 'No tears, everything's OK. And there's nothing kind about it. I care about you.'

'It's just ...'

He tipped my head up, with his fingers cupped over my ears. 'Just what?'

I looked up into his face and could see a faint reflection of myself in his glasses. 'It's been a long time since anyone was as nice to me as you are.'

'I'm sure it isn't, it's just the first time you've noticed for a while.'

I shrugged, a little childishly, because maybe he was right. But even so, I was embarrassed by my tears. I didn't know what it was with the waterworks lately. A combination of stress, exhaustion and fear I guessed.

I tried to turn away, but he held my head securely.

'What the hell did this Michael bloke do to you?'

OK, now that was dangerous tear territory and not something I talked about. 'Nothing.'

'Nothing? He must have done something. You were

215

like a deer caught in headlights just at the thought of a date with me.'

'I wasn't.'

He raised his eyebrows in a way that said I couldn't persuade him to think otherwise. And what was the point? He was right. A date was the first step in a relationship, and relationships were scary. The thought of having my soul shredded from my body again wasn't particularly appealing; to be honest, it was downright terrifying.

But even so, Carl deserved the truth. More than anyone he'd persevered with me. He'd forgiven, trusted and treated me with respect. I supposed he really did need to know what the hell he was getting himself into if this was going to be more than friendship.

'OK.' I took his hands from my head, linked my fingers with his and held them between our bodies. 'You really want to know?'

'Yes,' he said quietly. 'I do.'

'He really did nothing, literally. He just left. I came back from work, a day shift actually, that was before I went nocturnal, and he'd ... gone.' I paused, waiting for the usual stab of pain at the memory of walking through the door, calling to him that I'd splashed out and bought steak and a bottle of red on the way home, as it was a Friday. He hadn't replied and I'd thought he was in the shower or something. He wasn't.

'Gone?' Carl said, tilting his head. 'What do you mean?'

'He'd left a note, saying that he didn't love me any more. Didn't want to get married and he had an urge to travel the world while he was still young enough to do it.'

'And you had no idea he was feeling like this?' Carl shook his head. I could sense his confusion, his struggle to comprehend; it was like everyone else had been at the time.

'No, not at all.' I glanced away. 'We'd been out the night before, to the cinema, came home, made love and then enjoyed breakfast together. I thought he was happy, like I was. Truth be told, I was more than happy. I spent the first two years living in this flat with Michael, feeling like I was the luckiest woman on earth and walking on cloud nine all day every day.'

Carl looked bemused. 'And he hadn't said anything. Not even hints of travelling and stuff?'

'No, Michael is a Yorkshire lad, born and bred. Yorkshire men tend to be homebodies, they don't get the wanderlust other people do, and who can blame them? It's beautiful here.'

'Yes, but ...' He squeezed my fingers. 'But you just don't do that, do you? Walk away from someone you love.'

'He didn't love me.'

'But he proposed. Bought this place with you.'

I sighed. 'Yes, I agree the signs were there that he loved me. Maybe he did, maybe he didn't. But his actions undermined my ability to trust, to believe in my skills in judging how people felt about me.' I nodded at the cream pile rug in front of the fireplace. 'Have you any idea how many nights I lay on there sobbing, wondering what the hell I'd done wrong or what signs I hadn't picked up?' I pulled in a deep, shaky breath. 'Over and over I asked myself why he'd left in such a cruel way, no explanation, no chance for me to defend myself or try to make things right. The only contact I ever had with him was through a solicitor to sort out the deeds to this place. He took himself off the mortgage and I bought him out. I had some crazy idea in my head that if I kept our home together he might come back.'

An image of myself, what I must have looked like on that rug sprang to mind. I'd been boneless with grief. Michael leaving had been the most awful thing to ever happen to me. If he'd died in an accident it would have been easier. I wouldn't have had the questions, the uncertainties, the damn hang-ups I was now making every nice, innocent guy I met cope with. Talk about baggage, I had a bloody ten ton truck trailing along behind me.

'I don't want to think of you like that,' Carl said, turning me to face him and running his hands over my shoulders and down my arms. 'Perhaps we should make new memories for that rug.'

'New memories?'

'Yes.' He brushed his lips over mine. 'Perhaps I should make love to you there – sweetly, gently, right now.'

That sounded like a damn good idea to my body, but my emotions stuttered.

He knew me too well, already. 'What?' he asked. 'You've changed your mind?'

I looked away. Damn, I was such a tease. I did want to, really I did. But ...

'Hey,' he said. 'It's OK, whatever you want is fine.' He paused. 'I don't really know what's going on in that pretty little head of yours, but if it helps, I promise, absolutely promise, on my grandparents' graves that I will never ever just leave, walk away, or disappear. Ever.'

'You promise?' I looked up into his face. It was full of earnest, his jaw set, his eyes solemn.

'I promise, with all my heart. I would never do that to you, or anyone. It's just cruel. Unbelievably cruel.'

'It is.' I nodded. 'It was.'

He gathered me close, tucking my head beneath his chin and stroking my hair. I leaned into him, let him hold me up. I was knackered, emotionally and physically, almost to the point where Carl was keeping me together.

I slid my hands down his back, to just below the waistband of the smart trousers he wore for work. The rise of his buttocks was a gentle slope and like the rest of him, slender but strong.

Letting my palms absorb the heat of his skin through

219

the material, in this slightly too familiar pose for a couple yet to make love, I allowed the first stirrings of desire to build within me. It was new, this desire. It wasn't lust or a craving for physical satisfaction, which were the sexual emotions that had been with me for so long. It was something more brilliant, brighter, deeper. It came from within, an urge to connect in every sense, not just our bodies but as two souls. Not since Michael left had I felt that, not since Michael had I allowed myself to.

But maybe those years banging around weren't wasted ones though. Perhaps they'd been necessary. Kind of like an Elastoplast around my heart. Yes, I'd shagged any willing guy, been more than happy to reap the benefits of Raif's multi-talented tongue and ridden Tom's mammoth appendage until I could barely walk, but I'd never been truly satisfied. Hadn't come away feeling as though my heart had been nourished by the joining, no matter how spectacular the orgasm or how many I'd been treated to.

However, now, just holding Carl, and feeling him cuddle me was more nurturing than any fleeting rendez-vous. He knew me. Had seen me up and down. He understood that I was a sucker for patients who needed a night out and thought it enormous fun to watch senior colleagues up to no good in theatre. He also grasped, though many men wouldn't, that I'd had a sudden change of heart when just about to get up close and personal with Javier. Yes, he knew me, and now I wanted to learn everything about him too.

'You OK?' he whispered.

I nodded, inhaled his cologne. 'Yes, I'm fine.' I looked up at him. 'The rug is a little uncomfortable. How about the bed?'

He grinned. 'Sounds good to me.'

With a sudden flourish he swooped me up against his chest. One arm behind my knees the other around my back. I laughed, a bubbling rush of a sound, and looped my arms around his neck.

'I've been wanting to do that for ages,' he said with a smile. 'Sometimes I've looked at you on a ward, busy organising meds or helping someone out of bed, and I've wondered what you'd say if I just strode over, picked you up and marched out of the place.'

'You have?'

'Yes.' He walked into the hall, turning sideways to fit us both through the doorway. 'I always liked that film *An Officer and a Gentleman*; thought they should remake it though, *The Doctor and the Nurse*.'

'I think they have, and you can find it on the top shelf of sleazy, over-eighteen-only shops.'

He laughed. 'Yes, you're probably right.' He paused. 'Which one?'

'Door on the left, the other one is the bathroom.'

'OK, I'll remember that for later.'

221

He shoved at my bedroom door with his foot, and I was relieved that I'd left the room relatively tidy. It was quite a decent size, with one purple wall behind the bed and the others silvery grey. The bedspread was also purple and held a stack of fluffy, decorative cushions.

He laid me down, carefully, then flicked on the bedside lamp. A warm, amber glow filtered over the bed and cast shadows around the chunky pine furniture.

'Much as I like these sexy pyjamas of yours,' he said, stooping and talking against my lips, 'they're going to have to come off.'

'That can be arranged, doctor, but I think you might have to lose your clothes first.'

He straightened. 'Ah, it's like that, is it?' He dragged his shirt over his head and I got my first look at his bare chest.

And a fine chest it was too – creamy skin, unblemished; dark, hard nipples; a whirl of black hair in the centre of his sternum; and subtly defined, squarish pectoral muscles. His body was long, his chest hair forming a neat, tantalising, lickable line right down to his navel before fanning out, over his taut belly and disappearing into his trousers.

It was the length of his body and limbs that so appealed to me. He wasn't all beefed-up muscle, bulging biceps and stacked six-pack. He was lean, strong, tall, perfectly formed and all male. He was Carl.

Without tearing my attention from him, I flicked the cushions to the floor and tossed back the duvet. After toeing off my slippers, I poked my feet beneath the cover. 'Coming in?' I asked with a grin.

He didn't return my smile. He'd pressed his lips together and hovered his fingers over his belt buckle.

'What?' I asked. A shard of fear sliced through my chest. Please don't run out on me. Not now. Not when I've just let you in.

'It's just …' he said quietly.

'What?' OK, now I was worried.

'It's just …' He twisted his mouth into a half smile. 'I just hope you like it, that's all.'

I frowned. 'Like what?'

'I've been told it's a bit of an acquired taste.'

'Acquired taste.' I was really confused. 'Carl, what are you talking about?'

'This.' He undid his buckle, slowly slipped it free, then undid his trouser button and zipper.

Bloody hell. What was going on? Was he of mammoth proportions like Tom? Perhaps he had a wiener and I'd have to find inventive ways to get off with him. No, I'd felt the damn thing in the cupboard after the Hartley and Emily show. It'd seemed of perfectly acceptable proportions then.

He shoved his trousers down to his ankles then kicked them and his socks away.

OK, judging by the tenting in his tight, black boxer briefs, he definitely wasn't on the wiener end of the scale. That looked just as I remembered it to feel. A healthy, aroused specimen waiting for fun.

But this just made me even more puzzled. 'Carl,' I whispered. 'What –?'

'This.' He hooked his fingers into the waistband of his boxers and moved them down to his thighs. His cock sprang free from a nest of black pubic hair. He was a very pleasing length, decent girth and nicely engorged.

But as all of this registered, one thing overrode everything else.

'Bloody hell,' I gasped. 'Is that real?'

He gave a strained laugh. 'Yes.'

'What the ... why?'

'Why not?' He fingered the silver ring that emerged from his slit and then pierced the underside of his dick, just beneath the flared glans.

'I've never seen a Prince Albert,' I said, sitting forward. It looked amazing, the metal thick and shiny and kind of pretty too. 'And I thought I'd just about seen everything.'

'Does it freak you out? I can remove it if you want.'

'No, no, not at all.' I glanced up at his worried face. 'I think it's bloody amazing.'

He widened his eyes. 'You do?'

'Yes, how long have you had it?'

'About seven years. Had it done in Australia when

224

a mate dared me to. Hurt like bollocks for a while but then I got used to it, fond of it. Now it's part of me.'

'Remind me never to dare you to do anything.'

He laughed. 'Yes, I'm not good at turning a dare down. You'd do well to remember that.'

I grinned. 'I will.' Damn, I'd always suspected Carl was a dark horse beneath his white coat, square glasses and easygoing ways. I'd been right, and it seemed my luck just kept going up now that it had changed its course. 'Can I touch it?'

He released the ring and the small ball-bearing hung towards the floor, though his cock stayed proudly upright, pointing at my face. 'That's kind of the idea,' he said in a low, sexy voice.

'It is?'

He cupped my cheek in his palm. 'Yes. And when it touches you, inside – trust me, it will feel incredible. It'll hit just the right place.'

'How do you know?' I asked a little cheekily.

He licked his lips, grinned. 'Because I passed my female anatomy class with flying colours. I know exactly which hot spots will make you feel great.'

I glanced up at him and saw desire, anticipation and affection in his expression. I was aware of an expansion in my chest, like a balloon growing. It was desire, too, but a desire to satisfy him not myself. For too long I'd been taking what I could from sex and not reciprocating.

I juddered in a breath. I'd been a bit of a cow, probably. Using men for one thing only. But I'd always been honest about it. Never offered, promised or suggested more.

But this was different. I wanted to make Carl feel good – more than good. I wanted to hear him call out in ecstasy. Writhe with pleasure on the bed. Struggle to catch his breath because I'd taken him to such a soul-twistingly erotic place. And I wanted to see his face, with his eyes screwed tight, his nose wrinkled and his teeth gritted, battling not to give into his orgasm until he was ready to.

Carefully I placed my hands on his hips, leaned to the edge of the bed and swiped my tongue over the ring. Very gently, just enough to shift it slightly.

'Fuck,' he gasped, squeezing my shoulders.

I drew my tongue in, tasted sporty shower gel along with a musky metallic flavour.

'Is it OK to do that?' I asked, adoring the way the ring circled into his dark-pink slit.

'Yes, that's fine.' He sounded a little strained. His throat tight.

I repeated the action, then swirled my tongue under the rim of his glans. Exploring every smooth, stretched section of flesh and the small, tight dart of flesh a fraction above where the ring entered beneath the crown.

He groaned, a long, low rumbling sound.

Cupping his soft sacs, I took him completely into my

mouth, letting the smooth, cool metal of the ring slide on my tongue as I went deep, then deeper still.

'Sharon, please ...' He stepped back and I was forced to release him.

'What.' My breaths were coming quickly, my heart rate picking up. I was just about to get into a rhythm.

'I've been thinking about this moment with you for too long. Any more of that and I won't have an ounce of stamina left.'

'So just go with it,' I said, reaching for him again.

He moved to the left. 'I at least want to make it into the damn bed.'

I grinned. 'Yes, good idea.'

I flicked back the duvet and he slipped in next to me.

'So how come you're still wearing this?' he asked, curling his fingers beneath my fluffy top.

'I think you're very capable of treating that symptom, doctor.'

'Yes, I also happened to come top of the class in removing girly pink pyjamas.'

I giggled. 'That's good to hear.'

He tugged my top and I raised my arms, allowing it to slide over my head. Two seconds later it landed on the pile of cushions.

'Sharon,' he said, gazing at my breasts. 'You're beautiful.'

He'd said the words, but there was something in his

face that told me he meant it, truly meant it. His eyes were wide behind his glasses, his mouth soft, and there was a rise of colour on his cheeks.

I rested back on the pillow, as though offering myself up for him. He took the invitation, palming my right breast and leaning forward to kiss my nipple.

I slotted my hands into his hair, sighed and luxuriated in the feel of him suckling gently, stroking the nub with his tongue and massaging my flesh, testing out the weight and feel of me in his hand.

The need to have him inside me was there, definitely, but oh, it was lovely not to be rushing. To have the time and privacy to just sprawl out on the big soft bed, in the warm, and enjoy Carl enjoying me. There was nothing and no one else to worry about. It was as though there was just us in the world, in the universe.

He moved over me, his face hovering above mine and his hands on the pillow either side of my head. His glasses were much more than off a squint now, they were at a forty-five degree angle to his eyes and looked quite comical.

I reached for their thin black arms and slid them off. Carefully folded and set them on the bedside locker. I looked back up at him. It was the first time I'd ever seen him without his glasses. I liked it, a lot. He really was very handsome; proud, straight nose, angled jaw and cobalt-blue eyes that were all the more vivid against his spiky black lashes and dense eyebrows.

'Can you see me?' I asked, pushing his mussed up hair from his brow.

'You're a little bit soft-focused.'

'Just as well you said I was beautiful with your glasses on then.'

'It would still be true,' he said, touching his lips to mine. 'Because I meant inside and out.'

'You're such a softie.' I smiled against his mouth.

'Actually feeling quite hard right now.'

I giggled. 'Good.'

He explored my ribs, belly and hips with deft, sweeping strokes and then pushed at the waistband of my pyjama bottoms. Together we shoved until the pink material was bunched at the base of the bed. His bare hips and legs felt big and hard next to mine, his body hair a little tickly.

'I need a condom,' he said, kissing across my cheek to my temple.

His breaths were hot and loud, music to my ears. I ran my hands over his shoulders, skimming the arch of my foot down his calf to his heel. 'Mmm.'

'Condom,' he said again.

His skin was so warm and smooth, and his weight just lightly pressing me into the bed was divine. I bowed my back, pushed my nipples into his chest and ran my tongue over the angle of his jaw; the scratch of his stubble drew an appreciative moan from my throat.

'Condom,' he said more firmly. 'Now.'

229

'What? Oh, yes.' I fumbled blindly to my left. Yanked at the drawer and felt around until I found one. 'Here.'

He took it, sat back on his heels and proceeded to carefully unfurl the latex over his piercing. 'A bit tricky the first few times,' he said a little breathlessly. 'But I've got the hang of it these days.'

'I can see that.'

Once the condom was completely rolled down he nudged my legs apart and settled between them.

I opened willingly and reached for his shoulders. He prodded at my pussy and I tilted my hips impatiently. I was wet and hot, and when he reached down and slid his fingers through my folds and into my entrance, I clenched around him.

'Carl,' I said, just needing his name on my lips as I experienced this first, intimate moment.

'I want to touch you,' he whispered. 'But I want to make love to you too.'

'We've got all day,' I said, 'we can cover all bases.'

A muscle flexed in his jaw. 'Yes, you're right.'

He withdrew his fingers. I moaned a complaint, but then what I needed most was there, pressing into me.

Damn, he felt good, and I could feel the cool lump of the metal.

Staring up into his face, I rested my hands on his cheeks. I had a sudden need to look into his eyes as he penetrated me. No longer a nameless sex act, this was what I was ready for again. It had been so long since I'd had an emotional connection with someone I was letting into my body. Too long.

Thank goodness that was all about to change. I may have been broken beyond repair if Carl hadn't insisted I give him more than a quickie in the cupboard. A wave of gratitude washed over me. He'd saved me from myself. I'd been on a mission to starve my soul of love. Self-destruct.

Where would that have got me?

Nowhere.

I thought of Ted, injured and alone. I didn't want that solitary life, no way. I wanted heart-stopping, jump-off-a-cliff-for-you love. Till death do us part, richer for poorer, hold-you-until-the-end-of-time love. I'd had it and it had been taken away, but I was ready to try again. I had to. There was really no choice.

A lump of emotion caught in my throat. I opened my mouth to speak but couldn't form words.

Carl pushed in a little further. I gasped and that lump juddered out into the air between us.

He froze. 'You OK?' He bit at his bottom lip as if harnessing his willpower.

'Yes, fine.'

Although I didn't say it, he seemed to sense this was special on lots of levels for me. He locked his arms either side of my head, kept steady eye contact and seated fully inside me.

'Oh, oh,' I gasped, bending my knees and wrapping my lower legs around the backs of his thighs. 'Oh, that feels good. You feel good.'

'Tell me about it.' He was still gazing at me, barely blinking.

I smoothed my hands down the column of his neck then back up to his face. I wanted to touch him everywhere at once but didn't know where to start. 'Carl.'

'Yes.'

He pulled almost out and eased back in. My G-spot received a delectable long, firm stroke, not just from his cock but also from that wicked piercing. His pubic bone rubbed against my clit, sparking the swollen bud to life and making me instantly greedy for more.

A tremor ran up my spine, and my breasts felt heavy and aroused. 'That promise,' I managed.

'What about it?'

'You did mean it, didn't you?'

'Yes, absolutely. I want this. I want you. Not just in bed but in my arms, my life, for as long as you'll let me.' He kissed me, deep and profound, weaving his tongue with mine and feeding me his desire. 'Dare me to stay and you've got me until you dare me to go.' He managed a strained little smile.

'I don't want you to go.' To prove my point I clung to him tighter, succeeding in heightening the already intense sensations. 'I really don't want you to go. Stay, I dare you to stay.'

'Then just watch me.' He clenched his teeth, hissed in a breath. 'Fuck, I'm nearly there. You're amazing wrapped around me, fucking amazing. I feel like we've had months of foreplay.'

'It's just about driven me crazy with longing sometimes.'

'That could tip me over the edge just hearing you say that.' The tendons on his neck stood out as he lifted his head; there was a tiny drop of sweat in the hollow of his throat.

A shiver of bliss raced through me. This was how I'd wanted to see Carl, hear him, feel him. At war with himself and pleasure. The need to give in almost winning the need to continue with the build up. And all because of me.

Luckily my build up was almost at its height too. 'Don't stop, don't stop,' I gasped, bucking my hips to enjoy each one of his firm glides. 'I'm gonna be coming soon. That Prince Albert is sinfully good.'

'You like it?'

'More than like. It's amazing.'

We met each other, firm deep thrust for firm deep thrust, the sound of our breaths loud over the scrape of our pubic hair brushing. Our sweat-slicked bodies smoothed over one another in an erotic dance we'd perfected on the first try. We continued to gaze at each other; it was such a bare-boned, terrifyingly honest thing to do. Part of me wanted to glance away but I didn't dare break the spell. Spoil the moment or be the one to throw in the towel.

Suddenly it was there. My orgasm had built fast and solid and crashed down quicker and harder. His scandalously placed piercing, combined with his insanely skilled hips had thrown me over the edge and left me to spiral out of control.

'Oh, God, I'm coming,' I managed to gasp, a split second before the air trapped in my lungs and stayed there.

I hung on that precipice of extreme pleasure, the ultimate sensation, trying to prolong it and not once did I break eye contact. And then I was flung every which way. My pussy clamping hard, over and over, bliss darting like wildfire through my body. My clit was humming with pleasure as he bashed into it with a sublime pressure.

My toes curled, I dug my fingers into his shoulders, and arched my spine. I couldn't remember ever coming so hard. So beautifully, or so totally. Every nerve in my body exploded and, all the time, Carl held me together.

'Ah, baby,' he gasped. 'You done?'

I managed a brisk nod.

The controlled rhythm switched, suddenly, dramatically. One, two, three, fast, furious thrusts and then he was groaning through his release. Riding hard as he filled the condom and rammed so deep his balls crashed up against my buttocks.

He screwed his eyes up and his lashes knitted together.

I lifted my head and claimed his mouth.

He was passive to my kiss for a second or two then returned it hungrily. His whole body concrete beneath my hands. Hard, shaking, concrete.

'Ah, that was so intense,' I gasped as his shuddering eased.

A fraction of the tightness left his body and he dropped his weight to his elbows. 'Intense is one word, I suppose.' He paused to drag in air. 'A few others I can think of … just off the top of my head … fucking awesome … bloody brilliant … seriously sensational.'

I slept all day in Carl's arms, my head nestled in the crook of his shoulder, my legs kind of flung over his, but tangled too. I could feel his heartbeat beneath my palm. Slow, steady, reassuring, and although I was sleeping I was still aware of it, even in my dreams.

When I'd last slept with someone, as in literally, closed my eyes and let my brain drift through REM cycles, I couldn't remember. Well, that wasn't true, I could. It had been that very last night with Michael, after we'd been to see the Julia Roberts romcom.

But not any more. Now I'd slept with Carl.

As soon as I became aware of the room I knew it was late. The sunshine dribbling weakly through the gap in the curtains was definitely a pre-evening glow, darkness the only thing coming next.

A glance at the digital clock told me it was a little after five. Later than normal for me to sleep on a workday.

'Hey, you.'

I twisted my neck to look up. Felt the skin on my face peel from Carl's shoulder and knew my cheek would be creased and lined. Not attractive.

'Did you sleep well?' he asked, moving a lock of my hair that was dangling over my eye.

'Yes, really well. Guess that sleep injection helped.'

He laughed and my body jigged with the rise and fall of his.

'Glad to be of service,' he said. 'You want some coffee?'

'Yes, please. Sounds great.' I shifted to the right and flopped onto a cool section of sheet.

'Coming right up.' He stood and stretched in a totally unself-conscious way with his back to me.

Damn, he had some fine bum cheeks going on. Pert and dented on the outer edges. Yum.

'Sugar?' he asked, reaching down for his boxers and giving me a completely sinful, but perfectly delicious view.

'Er, yes, one please.'

He turned and grinned. I knew in that instant my dark horse had truly charged out of the stable. Carl was going to be so much fun for a naughty nurse like me to play with.

He wandered out of the bedroom, humming an old Beatles tune and I glanced at my uniform, discarded over the dressing table chair. There was a flash of white sticking out of the pocket and I remembered the letter Iceberg had given me.

Quickly I retrieved it, and after plumping the pillows and sitting back on the bed, tore it open and began to read.

Dear Sharon Roane,
This letter is sent to you from the partnership of
Gorly and Rimes, of 46 Heatherstock Road,
Bingley, W. Yorks, and is to inform you of a gift
attached to your name.
It is with a matter of urgency we urge you to
contact us and provide your bank details so that
the sum of £10,000 can be placed in your account.
Naturally, this is likely to come as a shock so I
have added a personal letter, addressed to you but
given to us on instruction.
Yours sincerely
K. Gorly.

My dear Sharon,
I know this letter will come as a surprise to you,
though I very much hope a good one, so please
forgive me for the official way in which these
matters must be addressed.

We only met once, when I was scared and confused in hospital a few weeks ago, but you were so incredibly patient with me and your sweet nature and gentle words have stayed with me in a way that warms my soul.

Your heartfelt kindness is something I simply can't let slip through my fingers the way so many other things seem to these days. So I have had my solicitor, Mr Gorly, contact you with the intention of giving you a gift to express my gratitude.

I sincerely hope that you can accept the sum of a little over ten thousand pounds. This is the total of a small endowment that has matured and it would give me great pleasure to know that I've given it to someone with such a pure heart.

Please don't think that by taking this money you will leave me short. I was a successful businessman in the later half of my working days and I could give you much more, so that you never need work again. But it scares me to do so. For your destiny is to nurse, the same way fighting those blasted Germans was my destiny. So, I hope this money helps pay off some bills or upgrade your car so you are safe on the awful icy Yorkshire roads, or maybe even treats you to a holiday, some winter sunshine.

Whatever you do with it have fun, please remain

exactly who you are, doing what you do best.
And once again, thank you so much for your
kindness to a scared, old man.

Yours truly,
Reginald Watkins. VC

My whole body tingled, my eyes prickled. Dear Mr Watkins, I remembered him well, lying in bed, cold, scared and believing that the Germans were coming. He'd been much happier and more orientated by the time I'd moved to my next duties and left him warm and supping on sugary tea. He'd then had a good night's sleep and woken eager for the morning paper and marmalade on toast.

I shoved my hands into my hair, tipped my head to the ceiling and sucked in a deep breath. That wasn't a letter I ever thought I'd receive. I scrubbed at my eyes and then re-read the entire thing, from start to finish, and by the time I had, Carl was walking back into the bedroom holding two steaming mugs of coffee.

He stopped at the end of the bed.

'What's wrong?' The smile on his face fell.

'Nothing.'

'Something is.' He appeared frozen.

'Nothing, it's nothing. I've just had some rather amazing news. A letter.'

'Oh, yeah?' He set my coffee down.

239

'Yes, a patient, has given me ten thousand pounds.'

'What?' His own coffee started to tip and he quickly righted it. 'Ten grand? Bloody hell!'

'I know, it's amazing.' Actually, it was. And as I said it I realised just how amazing.

Ten thousand pounds!

I passed the letter to Carl. 'Read it.'

He sat on the bed, his back rod-straight against the padded headboard. I handed him his glasses and he rubbed his index finger on his bottom lip as he read.

'That's fantastic,' he said, shaking his head in amazement and passing the letter back to me.

'I know,' I said. 'I'm so happy.' I grinned, slightly manically.

'Put your coffee down.' His voice was suddenly low and deep.

'What?' My smile fell.

'You heard.' There was a steely look of determination in his eye.

'Er ... OK.' I set the mug aside.

Suddenly I was on my back, looking up into mesmerising blue eyes and feeling his weight spread over me. 'Carl!'

'Seems everyone that meets you falls in love with you ...' He paused. 'Including me.'

'Carl, I ...'

'Which leaves me with one question.' He touched his lips to mine. 'Do you think you could ever fall in love with me?'

Fears and hopes tumbled together, the desire to protect my vulnerable heart as strong as the need to set it free. Could I deny the truth? Was I going to allow myself to be exposed to potential hurt again and fall in love with Carl? It was a risk, a big risk.

But I knew the answer to his question. It was actually pretty easy. A decision that had made itself. 'I think I'm already falling in love with you,' I said. I looked deep into his eyes and then kissed him.

He kissed me back with a hunger I could happily live with forever. 'I won't let you down,' he whispered. 'I promise.'

'Good, I'm trusting you. I haven't trusted anyone in a very long time.'

'I know, and I will treasure that trust and treat it with great care. I'll wrap it in cotton wool and put it in a secure box, look after it very carefully and help it grow strong again.'

I sighed and held him tight, loving having another person in my arms, my bed and my life. Someone who understood me, even if they didn't know every little thing about me. And someone who I got, whose layers were open and honest, even if there were some I was yet to have the pleasure of discovering.

'So we're really going to do this?' he said, kissing across my cheek and sliding his hand over my right breast.

'Yes.'

'And I can tell people that you're my girl.' He travelled his kisses down my neck.

'If you really want to start that rumour off.'

He ducked to gently flick his tongue over my nipple. 'But it's not a rumour, it's true.'

I smiled and stroked his hair. 'Yes, and I'm more than happy that it's true. Let's shout it from the highest hill and scratch it onto the rocks of the deepest valley.'

And I was happy. With my financial fortunes turned, Iceberg gone and a new, seriously sexy man in my life, I suddenly had a vibrant, alive future to look forward to, one that seemed all the brighter for having been in a dark, lonely place for such a long time.

But would I stay nocturnal?

Yes, probably, for a while at least. There was always so much more fun to be had in the still of the night. When the corners were shadowy, the frantic buzz of the day asleep like a fractious monster waiting to wake, and the patients prepared to reach out for what they really needed.

That was my world, the night time; it was where I belonged and where I was happy doing what I did best, nursing. Though now any mischievous shenanigans in linen cupboards or on-call rooms would only involve Carl, the man who'd not only diagnosed my broken heart but had also been the rather delicious cure. Who said medicine didn't taste good? Mine was truly scrumptious!

www.ingramcontent.com/pod-product-compliance
Ingram Content Group UK Ltd.
Pitfield, Milton Keynes, MK11 3LW, UK
UKHW022302180325
456436UK00003B/183